Das Herz:

Buch Eins

Das Herz:
Buch Eins

By Sayda Hope

This is a work of fiction. Names, characters, places, and all other details are the product of the author's imagination. Any similarities are purely coincidental.

Das Herz: Buch Eins © 2019 by Sayda Hope

Cover Design by Sayda Hope and illustrated by Viktoriia Boiko

ISBN # 978-1-7331924-2-2 (paperback)
ISBN # 978-1-7331924-3-9 (e-book)

KAPITEL I

Wierderganger - Of Germanic origin, meaning "Again Walker". Tales of the dead rising have been told for centuries. Associated with plagues, mysterious deaths and even weather changes, their existence in stories is usually vengeful, sexual, or are merely depicted as nightmarish monsters that survive on an unholy hunger. The reason for a person to awaken from the dead could be the result of nearly anything, ranging from not having their names removed from the burial clothes to dying in battle. Remedies for these lurking creatures varied from driving a stake with one thrust into the mouth, binding the head to the ground beneath it, or forcing a stone into its jaws, keeping it from biting. All the cultures of the world have their own versions of the undead... some are simply more frightening than others.

Snowy rain and blinding fog, such is the usual here. The Trennt Mountains have been the sight of battle. A battle that has left thousands dead, both ally and enemy.

In the early evening, a Commanding Officer approaches a large hillside camp on horseback in a light snowfall. His uniform is adorned with such honors that it is easy to tell that he is a high-ranking officer, yet still active in battle. Riding with him is a small group of fellow soldiers meant as reinforcements. Their number is a quarter of the soldiers already at the camp. The Commander halts at one of the resident officers of the camp and begins to dismount his horse. The officer is an average sized man with good looks but no appearance of the roughness about him that is usually seen in soldiers.

"Sir," the younger man greets as the Commander passes him and makes his way into the biggest tent meant specifically for him. Upon entering the tent, the Commander picks up a glass and pours a drink for himself. "It is good to have you here, Sir," the young man tells the General. "When Captain Amory was killed in battle, command fell to me, but I felt this conflict was important enough to require the guidance of an officer as... experienced as you," the man says standing at attention.

The General turns, still with drink in hand. "Sending word for me was the right thing..." he wonders the younger man's name.

"Mikhail Koza, Sir."

"So tell me Koza, what do you think of this enemy army that killed your Captain?" the General asks calmly.

Still at attention, he replies, "They are… sturdy," wanting to choose the right word.

"Do you know the name of their Commander?"

"Brigadier General Eber Soldat… Sir."

The Commander's grip on his glass tightens as he thinks of the weight that name carries. He looks back up at the officer. "Not many have survived confrontations with Soldat. His mind is honed for war," the General starts to leisurely walk around the table serving as a desk. "How long have you been at this stalemate with his army?"

"The last conflict was before word was sent to you, Sir." The General glances to the ground, seemingly lost in thought. "What are you thinking, Sir?"

"I heard he is the relentless type. It's quite strange he has not attacked again."

Abruptly, there is a call from outside the tent and another soldier enters hastily, the urgency pushing aside any need for permission. "Commander." Koza turns to the young soldier who is half his size in girth and muscle.

"What is it?" the General asks.

"There is a man approaching… It is Soldat."

"Soldat?" the Commander looks puzzled. Immediately, he leaves the tent, walking past Koza. "What does this mean?"

As the Commander passes through the flap of the tent, he steps out among his soldiers. Unable to see more than a Der Vorfahr soldier hopping down from his horse, the Commander watches his men gather around the couple of horses. Gradually, the men begin to move back, making a path as another Der Vorfahr soldier comes forward.

Somewhat entranced by the myth walking towards him, the commander stares at the warrior, the falling snow in the mountains speckling his black uniform of cloth and leather. Leather the commander recognizes as a different pattern than the other soldiers.

Under the fundamental threat of a Der Vorfahr soldier, the black uniforms, the weapons forged of strong metals, the combat training that mixes brute muscle with well-thought plans and tactics, there is a threat to this man all its own. His dark eyes stay fixed on the Commander with such a calmness that one would never think those eyes had seen war, seen bloodshed, or pained deaths of men. His pace, a steady one, as though he was the maker of time, instead of victim to it. His air, as though it were his own camp he walks into, rather than an enemy's.

The last of this man's threat is his sword. The Commander briefly looks at it, examining the weapon as he approaches. Different from any metal of Der Vorfahr, Soldat's sword holds the Commander's gaze. The long sword worn loosely at his hip is oddly different from most he has seen. The long thin handle ended with a round silver pommel, the crossguard, and two curved pieces of silver tipped by their own round balls.

Soldat steps up to the Commander and speaks, "Lieutenant General Borvo Larkonov?" his Germanic tone is rich with power and smooth with control.

After the General's comprehending pause at the idea of having this man right in front of him, Larkonov replies, "Yes, and you are Brigadier General, Eber Soldat?" the ominous man gives silence as his reply. "I must say, it is quite something to have you here before me. With all the stories I heard of you, I was beginning to think you were not a man of flesh and blood," he says, fully aware that he must keep his guard.

Soldat's manner is eerily tranquil as he simply answers, "I have heard little of you." Larkonov wrinkles his nose at the sedate insult. "What I have heard is that you are important... Valuable."

Said so plainly, the Commander's brows lower to meet the wrinkle on his nose, an uneasiness building in his gut. "Why are you here, Soldat?"

"…I am here to surrender."

The dazed Larkonov flinches and looks the man over for deception. "You? Surrender?"

"Shall we discuss terms?"

Larkonov turns to Koza, then proceeds to his tent. "Come this way." He halts suddenly, realizing Soldat would be at his back. Larkonov nods towards the tent entrance. "You first, General." Soldat moves into the tent. Koza enters last and closes the flaps of the tent to allow some privacy. He then walks over to Larkonov, standing ready to defend his Commander should Soldat attempt something. The enemy watches Koza, then looks back to Larkonov. "So what are the conditions of your surrender?"

Almost as if in a moment of pain, Soldat crosses his arms and folds his hands inward. "It is the Plague."

"There is a sickness through your camp?"

"It has eliminated nearly all of my army. The numbers have so vastly decreased that continuing to make a stand against you would be pointless."

An expression of confidence grows over Larkonov's face. "I see," he examines the desk and papers, discussing battle strategies resting on it. "I will accept your surrender then, and you shall bring the remainder of your surviving army here, the ones who are not sick."

"As you say," Soldat replies coldly.

"It is a pity that such a powerful battle figure as you has met defeat in such a pathetic way," Larkonov says with poise, almost having honesty in his tone. With the sound of metal hitting metal, there are sudden cries that reach through the tent. "What?!" Larkonov rushes toward the entrance, past Soldat who stands unmoving, his eyes setting on Koza. Shoving at the flap of the tent, Larkonov charges out to find the soldiers he was summoned to bring as reinforcements, all lying dead, the last one of them being cut down by one of the Der Vorfahr men. The soldier yanks his axe from the man's body, setting it to his broad shoulder and giving a grin to Larkonov. "What is this?! Why did you all do nothing?!" He growls at the camp of soldiers who stand, watching the site of their own being killed. Larkonov rages as the soldiers ignore his gesture and stand without taking any action. At this point, Soldat comes out of the tent and comes by the Commander as Koza follows suit. Fighting his frustration, the Commander begins to calm his nerves, examining the faces of the men around him. "Koza."

"Yes. Sir?" He answers, behind the two commanders.

"These are not Amory's men, are they?"

"...No, Sir."

"Neither are you?"

"...No, Sir."

Gliding his eyes to his side, his swallowed dread turns to Soldat. "It was you who sent the request for reinforcements? You, who said you wanted me to come?"

Rather emotionlessly, Soldat looks to Larkonov. "As I said, you are important."

Fully realizing the trap he has walked into, Larkonov makes his last request. "Would you let me pray?"

The familiar sound of metal being unsheathed answers the man. Soldat, drawing his sword, swings it with a pace defiant of the General's leisurely nature used in all else. Closing his eyes, Koza reopens them, hearing the thud to the ground. Blinking, he sees Larkonov's body lying, while his head rests a stride away from it. Koza lets out a breath, pity sounding in the puff of air.

Sliding his blade back into the sheath, Soldat crouches and picks up Larkonov's head by a clump of hair. "This war is now ended." He moves past Koza, aimed for the tent. Koza watches the Der Vorfahr soldiers disguised in enemy uniforms begin to cheer, while Ermanno swings his axe and chuckles.

"We killed the last great commander." Thayer approaches, looking over the body left behind in the snowy mud. "Like the Commander said, the war is over with Larkonov's death." The young soldier half Koza's girth in size and muscle smiles at his life-long friend. "It means we can go home, Mikhail."

Hearing the peace in his voice, Koza turns to Thayer, setting a hand gently on the blonde's shoulder with a soft rocking motion. "Yes, Johan, home." Thayer watches Koza turn away from him, with sadness on his face.

KAPITEL II

Ubour – Of Bulgarian origin. When the spirit of a person refuses to leave the body after death, that person awakens from that death after forty days have passed. The Ubour is not known to be picky in what it eats do to tales that speak of it being more interested in consuming the meat of living creatures than in feeding on blood.

Into the night, the hillside battlefield that was once boisterous with yells of fight, pain and death is silent. There is a quiet peace that flows through the camp, deeds done, battle won and tomorrow at dawn, it would be time to return home to Loviturä. Another icy rain storm is growing strength in the sky and plans to soon let loose on the earth.

Knocking at the wooden post of the Commander's tent, Koza awaits his permission. "Come." Entering into the tent, he finds Soldat lying atop the cot bed with hands over his stomach and eyes closed. The image that creeps its way into Koza's sight being that of Larkonov's head, resting upright on the desk.

"One would think that King Berin would believe you by now when you say you have killed the person he sent you to, and that you needn't bring him a head to prove it," Koza spouts, a lip over a tooth at the vile sight.

"Berin is a liar, he expects everyone else to be," Eber answers with eyes closed.

"That is very psychological." Koza sniffs.

A moment of silence passes, then Koza sniffs again. "What do you want?"

"You are a great commander. I would have no such certainty of victory under the leadership of another as I have under you. You are brilliant, you are strong and you are brave." Eber opens his eyes slightly at the cross points of the tent. "You are…"

"Koza, take care in your next choice of words because they had better have purpose," he says, not moving from his resting position.

"It is just that, because you are such a great leader, why must we resort to trickery?" he asks righteously.

"For the reason that it works."

"Yes, but Sir, to lure someone to their death when all the while you already know what you are going to do to them. Is it not…" Gradually, the young man's eyes move over Eber's sword leaning against the bed. The curves of cold steel, the sharp edges he knows rest inside its sheath, the lifelessness to the metal that takes life from others. He stares at the sword and sees his commander. "Wrong?"

"…You are a good man, Koza… I am not."

Softly, Koza replies, "Sometimes I wonder if you have ever had a heart, or if you have always been cold as your blade?" Eber's eyes drift to Koza. The young Captain smiles and nods. "Goodnight, Sir." He ducks his head and leaves the tent. Steadily, Eber's gaze lowers from the entrance to the sword by his side.

The second Koza steps outside, something catches his eye. A soldier is coming over a hill to the north through the dark and heavy woods. The soldier is wearing a tattered uniform of Der Vorfahr. He is an ally, but he is unrecognizable. His movements and posture seem to be with effort. First Lieutenant Thayer comes up to Koza's side, curious about the man as well. They look at one another and then Koza heads toward the man, thinking perhaps he is injured which would explain his slow, cumbersome walk.

When Koza reaches a shorter distance to the man, he calls out, "Soldier?" the man stops. There is no response. "Soldier!" The man's head quivers as if it strains to look up. In an instant, the man runs at Koza. His teeth are bared with a feral expression on his face. Koza draws his blade and with an easy strike, he drops the man to the ground. The man had put forth no defense, he simply charged without thought. Koza kneels down to have a better look at this creature. As Thayer watches this, Koza suddenly yells to him, "Get the Commander! Quick!"

Eber walks up to Koza who's still kneeling beside the man and stands looking down at them both. He quietly analyzes the being on the ground. He sees the man's face and eyes. The only question he asks is, "Where did it come from?"

Koza points to the northern treeline and Eber begins to walk toward it as Koza expresses his thoughts while still at the body. "It has teeth, strange teeth, sharp," he says nervously aware of what he is saying. "Its speed was not human, the way it moved, the way it looks is not human." Then, he notices the scar on the face, which strikes him cold. "Oh my God, it is Dieter!" he looks towards Eber, who is getting closer to the treeline. "Sir! Dieter died in battle, we buried him over a month ago!" he pauses, absorbing what he thinks this creature might be. "Sir, I think he is an untoter!"

Eber stops and pauses silently fifteen or more meters from the treeline, then turns back to the men in the camp, discussing all that has just happened with them. With force Eber barks, "Quiet!" the camp ceases its sounds immediately. Eber turns back to the forest devoting his attention to the smallest sound he might hear from it. Then as the hush of all noise settles in, there from deep into the woods close to the battlefield that laid undisturbed for days, comes a cry no man there had ever heard before. Powerful and sharp, not of human or animal. As the first cry dies down, the sound of countless others rise from the forest.

Eber turns hastily and heads back to the men in camp, knowing that the formation of a single unit will give the best chance. "Ready weapons!"

Eber draws his sword taking point. The diversity of his army's individual skills are expressed by Thayer's bow and arrow as well as his bizarrely thin blade retained for closer combat, and Ermanno's favored battle axe. Koza steps over to join his General, unsheathing his short blade perfect for swinging with ease in confined fighting conditions as glimpses of the creatures begin appearing through the trees.

They wear blood soaked, weapon torn uniforms of fellow soldiers and of the enemy. They are not moving as a unit or a pack, but are running with the seemingly single-minded drive of personal voraciousness. As they come from the forest, a rush of eminent doom can be felt, however, Eber's army is usually one of calmness and certain success as it is normally their own leader that inspires such feelings of fear and demise. In a state of waiting, Eber stands composedly, ready for the fight as an uneasy Koza turns back to the unholy horde and knows what is to come.

The attack begins, each man fighting his own war as the creatures spread through the camp. As there would be brief breaks from the fighting, Koza has the opportunity to gaze out at all that is happening. He sees Ermanno thriving against the beasts, in many ways actually enjoying the slashing and hacking, behavior not out of the ordinary for him. He looks to Thayer, his childhood friend who followed him to war years ago, not doing so well as the undead almost absurdly outnumber the living. When he glances at Eber, he sees the reputation of his Commander well at work, as he slashes at the creatures, cutting off their heads with single swipes.

As Eber swings his blade to the side after a strike, there is an unexpected approach of an untoter that carelessly thrusts itself onto Eber's sword, thereby killing itself. His blade becomes stuck in the lifeless beast. Unable to free his sword, he is now open to attack and a number of untoten take the chance given to them. Eber is thrown to the ground as the creatures overpower him. There is a moment of realization through the camp that Eber is being slain. Such a thing was never really thought possible. Happening so quickly, there is nothing that can be done say for halting momentarily in astonishment. Not able to see much more than his hand fall limp to his side, Koza and the rest of the soldiers know that with Eber Soldat's death, a fate of the same was now handed to them.

KAPITEL III

Hours now past, the untoten have long gone and the camp lay still as the icy rain drips from the sky. All are dead and the horses that had not been eaten by the creatures have run away. A scene expected to be bloody is quite the opposite. The creatures, having not only fed on the bodies, have lapped up much of the blood that had pooled on the ground as well. As the sun begins to rise and push back the rain, a crow soars overhead. It lands on the body of Koza and begins to peck at him, scavenging on what it can from his open wounds. Suddenly, Koza's hand comes up and grabs the crow, throwing it to the side. It lets out a caw and flies off. Koza sits up in bearable pain, his eyes blur as he looks over one dead body after another and begins to remember he should be no different. He rises slowly to his feet and sees Thayer coming to him in a similarly frayed and dazed state.

They stand, simply glaring at one another. "What has happened? Are we alive?"

Koza says haggardly to his old friend, "I do not think so."

Thayer looks out at the dead, then back at Koza. "Then we are die Untoten."

With fatigued hesitation, "We are the Undead," Koza replies nodding in agreement.

A brief distance from them, they hear the sounds of struggle. With a bit of effort, Ermanno pushes carcasses of the untoten off of him. He gets up as if he has been through a rough night of tavern escapades. "It figures he came back," Thayer says in ill humor.

Koza looks to see if others are rising, but detects no such thing. He turns to Eber, who lies prone on the ground. Koza walks to him and lowers to a knee. He sees the wounds on Eber, the worst being a virtual slit on his throat from tearing nails clawing at what they could. He looks at the lifelessness in Eber's eyes. "I would have thought if anyone were to return from the dead, it would be him," Koza states.

Ermanno comes to Thayer who is watching Koza. "Maybe he is just playing possum, poke him," Ermanno gestures with a grin.

"I am not going to poke the Commander!" Koza snaps back to him.

Koza stands up and looks down at his fallen leader. "Should we bury him?" Thayer asks.

"I will find a shovel," Koza replies and slowly walks back to the two men.

Ermanno slaps his hands on his stomach and proclaims chipperly, "I am hungry."

Thayer and Koza equally turn their attention to him and ask, "For what?"

Not quite knowing himself, Ermanno glances around, finally resting his line of sight on a nearby body. He steps over to it and kneels down, picking up the dead man's arm in his hands. He lowers his mouth to it and just as he is about to take a bite, he notices Thayer and Koza staring at him. "What?!... I am the undead! I'm going to Hell anyway."

Thayer looks away and in that second, he grabs Koza's arm. "Mikhail!" the men turn to see Eber lifting himself to a sitting position. Slowly, he starts to get up but appears unsteady. The men watch as Eber's movements are more like the first untoter that came to the camp.

"Commander?" Koza calls out. Eber stops moving without turning to face the men. Koza swallows forcefully, knowing that the Commander would not be nearly as easy to cut down as the first untoter was. "Eber?" the General turns and looks at the men. His eyes have an incoherent appearance as though he does not know who he is. In this moment, he is nothing more than a thoughtless creature of damnation. Steadily, Koza readies himself. "Men, I believe we are going to have to fight the Commander."

Thayer winces. "We are dead." Koza looks to the young man at his side. Feeling his eyes on him, Thayer replies, "I mean dead dead." Suddenly Eber disappears into thin air with a wave of vibration.

Collectively, the men gawk at the empty air where Eber was. "The others didn't do that!" Ermanno complains.

The men shoot their concentration everywhere trying to see him. Just then, Eber appears amongst them and throws Ermanno to the side with little effort, then slashes his nails at young Thayer. Koza rushes to help his friend who lies on the ground, unable to move without great pain from the gash. Koza drags the boy away from Eber just as the Commander stabs his claws into the dirt where Thayer's body was.

"Commander!" Koza tries to reason and is hit in the chest for it.

The force of the incoming blows throwing him back as much as the impact. The Captain scrambles for his sword that's been tossed farther than he. Aware of the Commander's fast approach, he searches desperately for something to use as a weapon. He sees the sword of his Commander that had been stuck in one of the undead creatures. A blade that possibly possesses as much reputation as the Commander himself. He whips round and points the blade at his leader. At once, Eber stops and stares at the blade. Koza wonders what is happening while he watches Eber remain still. There is no change of expression in his eyes or on his face, he simply seems frozen. Slowly, the Captain considers an idea which makes him tremble. He turns the blade in his hand and points the handle to his leader for him to take.

"Koza, are you out of your mind?!" Thayer yells.

"Quiet!" he barks back, not taking his eyes off the Commander. "No one say or do a thing," he pants. It is a last hope. A chance to bring back the leader's senses, when to fail means certain destruction. Calmly, Eber reaches for the sword and takes it. Pleased so far, Koza stands motionlessly, watching how the scenario will play out. Almost entranced, Eber straightens, staring down at the blade in his hand, when suddenly, Ermanno rushes Eber with his axe in hand. The Commander catches Ermanno by the throat, stopping him in an instant. Eber peers at Ermanno coldly. "You are planning on using your axe on me, Ermanno?"

Ermanno, taking the obvious hint that his Commander has regained his senses, tosses his weapon to the side. "What axe?" he chokes out the words with Eber's hand still round his throat.

The Commander releases him by means of dropping him to the ground causing a thud. Eber sheaths his sword and glances around the camp to inspect the damage. "You are yourself again, Commander," Koza remarks as he gets up and Thayer approaches.

While the Commander stands quietly starting to observe his body's new peculiarities, Koza, Thayer and Ermanno begin debating. "I feel so different now from when I was alive," Koza states.

Ermanno is sitting down leisurely on the ground with his arms resting on his knees. He looks up. "How so?"

"When I awoke from the dead, I felt… tired, hurt, but now that just a few moments have passed I feel strong."

Thayer looks to Koza. "Looks-wise we are the same. Our skin tones are the same, not pale like the dead. Our eyes are not black like demons."

Ermanno harasses, "That is not true. My nails are like claws and were not before. Moreover, the Commander's eyes are like a demon's, but they have always been that way." Eber glances back at Ermanno who spreads a pointy toothed grin.

"There is much I do not understand about what we are, but what I am finding most confusing is why have we maintained our wits about us, when all the untoten that attacked seemed like animals." Thayer finishes his thought.

"When the Commander awoke, he too was like the ones that attacked, but then he regained his mind. I am left to assume that it must depend on the individual?" Koza surmises to his best effort.

"How did the Commander regain his senses?" Thayer inquires.

"It had to do with seeing his sword. It appeared to make you remember something," he looks to the silent General. Staring out over the dead soldiers across the camp, Eber slowly lifts his arms, crossing them, as once more, a twinge wrinkles his brow slightly.

As if his attention is drawn by the sigh, Thayer turns to Koza. "So what is going to happen to us? What are we going to do?"

Koza replies in doubt, "I do not know. Perhaps, we will return to Muscovy?"

"I do not particularly care where I end up," Ermanno notifies. "Maybe I will venture to a small village," he wiggles his eyebrows up and down. "A defenseless village," He grins.

"We are returning to Loviturä," Eber commands drawing looks from his men.

"We are going back to Loviturä?" Ermanno asks.

"Sir, not that I doubt you," Koza raises his hands and looks submissively. "I just wonder, is it such a good idea to return to a heavily populated area like Loviturä?... We are the damned now."

Eber looks over at Koza, "We are no more damned now than we have always been." Koza blinks as he begins to understand how his Commander sees this. "You are thinking of us as monsters and forgetting your duties. No matter what we now are, firstly we are soldiers… that has not changed."

"Yes Sir," Koza replies obediently.

Eber looks ahead and says, "We are to return to Loviturä as though nothing has happened. And when some hunger or ability arises, it will be controlled, understand?" he looks to each man influentially.

"Yes Sir," Koza says with certainty.

"Yes Sir," Thayer follows his friend's lead.

Eber glances to Ermanno. "Of course," Ermanno says undevotedly. Eber holds his stare. "Yes Sir," succumbing to the Commander's governing essence.

Eber faces ahead and with every horse slain or run off, he contemplates the long walk home, the very long walk home. "I will get my head." He ventures for the destroyed tent where Larkonov's head was left, the men silently watching him in tandem.

KAPITEL IV

Strigoi Mort – Of Romanian origin. Said to be more akin
to a witch. This dangerous and ambiguous undead is
described as both human and demonic. If a person dies
without being married, is the seventh son of a seventh son,
or has sinned in life, they rise from their graves as a Strigoi
Mort. There are even legends of the creatures returning to
the lives they had with friends and family before death.
For example, a soldier who has died in war coming home.

After some days of travel, they stand on the hills to the south of Loviturä and stare down onto the large fortress city of their King. King Alaric Berin, ruler of Der Vorfahr, a country that spreads approximately 800,000 square kilometers. He is a man with nigh on 300,000 soldiers at his disposal and with the marriage to the Princess of Italy, Aletea Benesi, giving him more power and assistance when needed, he has been made a formidable man. In fact, the only resistance that has proven to be any challenge against him has been Ambrozij Kasimir, the head of the Christian church within Loviturä.

Eber looks up from the King's castle of Reinhard that lay right before them, from where the bulk of the castle is nestled among the mountainous hills of the south, across the city to the church. Reinhard, resting on one border of Loviturä and the church resting on the opposite one, entices a feel of rivalry. Taking into account the looks of each impressive force, it makes the feeling even stronger.

Reinhard is a castle of width rather than height, built with sturdy grey stones brandished by time with chips, gouges and deep scratches not giving testament to weakness, but inspiring resilience. It is scarred the same as many of the warriors who have defended it.

The church, however, is made of new white stone and rises to the heavens of the one it is meant to worship, ever expanding and growing. It is a might that has long since begun its encroaching assault.

Eber knows that what he and his men now are must be kept secretive. No one must know they are the undead or they will meet a death they will not return from by the hands of not God, but Ambrozij Kasimir, a man who desires to be one.

They begin to make their way down onto the grounds of the castle that in places branches out into the city, but mostly is a community unto itself. It is a society of soldiers and servants as well as other lower status individuals. The surrounding grounds of the castle offer practically all the conveniences of the city, food, lodging, drink, further instilling the notion of keeping the insignificant from the higher society of the city.

Having entered the grounds of the castle they are in familiar territory, they walk through the narrow streets, passing by blacksmiths that forge and repair swords as well as tend to horse tack and wagons. They pass by merchants that cater sales only to soldiers. "People are staring at us, do you think they can sense something?" Thayer asks, leaning over to Koza.

In a hushed voice Koza replies, "They are not staring at us, Johann. They are staring at the head." The severed head of Larkonov sways in Eber's grasp at his side.

Ermanno sets his hands to his hips. "You would think they'd all be used to seeing the Commander hauling around a severed head by now." Koza and Thayer glance back at the man, then run into the back of Eber who has stopped unexpectedly.

Eber turns and faces the three men. "You are to appear as though everything is normal and continue with your usual behaviors so that no suspicion is drawn. However, you are not to eat or drink anything. I have no idea how food or drink will affect us." His orders always having a relaxed tone, but a commanding presence just the same.

"Yes Sir," Koza says, as a collective response for the three.

Eber pauses a moment. "Also..." he begins to walk in between Thayer and Koza and steps up directly in front of Ermanno. "Because I do not know exactly what type of undead we are, there will be no sexual consorting with the living." He turns and begins to walk away towards the castle, able to be seen from the merchants' courtyard where they are. "Children are Hellspawn as they are."

Koza and Thayer watch him leave. "I will make certain to keep Ermanno out of trouble Sir!" Koza states with Eber getting out of sight. Then, Koza and Thayer turn back to Ermanno only to find him missing. "Der'mo!"

A man servant walks into a large room with a high ceiling. He pushes the heavy doors open, letting in light from the torches lining the endless network of hallways outside. The only other light in the room besides what has crept in from the hall as the man leaves the doors open, is the fire in the hearth. Every one of the hundreds of fireplaces in the castle is enormous in order to stave off the cold of its stone. There are only two chairs in the room and they are occupied by the King and Queen who are sitting by the fire.

The man stops at least ten meters from the Royals. "My King." The man bows deeply.

King Berin turns a lazy gaze to the servant, as does the Queen with book in hand. "What is it?"

"Brigadier General Soldat has returned from battle."

With excitement, Berin replies, "Wonderful, show him in, quickly!" when the servant leaves, a moment passes where Eber walks into the room and up to Berin and his wife. He does not bow. "You had success?"

"Yes."

"Amory is dead?"

"Yes."

"And Larkonov?" Berin questions, knowing the importance of those two men in his desire to take over more lands.

His answer is the toss of Larkonov's head onto the floor between the chairs. Dropping the book, the Queen shrieks, slapping her palm over her mouth in horror. At the same sight, King Berin begins to smile. "Very good." Queen Aletea watches Berin grin with disgust. He motions to the servant. "Clean that up." Eber turns and starts to walk out. "Eber?" He halts as the servant rushes behind him toward the head. "Before you settle in for the evening and think you can get some rest, I have another task for you." Vacantly, Eber stares at the doors to the room, his back still at the King, the fire, and the servant picking up the fire-tongs in try to fetch the severed head with the tool rather than hands. "In the southeast, about 560 kilometers away, there is a village named Hieb. I am giving you the assignment of a guard detail. You will select a few of your men and protect the travelers on the journey to Hieb."

"Whom am I guarding?"

The servant scurries away with the head in the tongs, rushing by Eber out the door. "Ambrozij Kasimir and possibly a couple of his priests," Berin tells.

"...Kasimir?"

"Yes," Berin smirks. "Something about blessing the village or some blather." He rubs at his Jaw as Aletea picks up her book, the head's leave putting her at ease once more. "To be honest, if you and I know Kasimir, we can assume there is perhaps another reason he wishes to go to Hieb. And, you and I do know him well, do we not?" He gives a chuckle.

"When do I leave?"

"You may rest if you wish and leave the day after tomorrow... I do not mind making the Head of the Church wait." Berin picks at a finely buffed nail. "It helps remind

him who is really King." In silence, Eber continues out of
the room.

In the meantime Koza and Thayer find themselves at a
tavern in the merchants' courtyard. When Koza opens the
door, a chair abruptly comes flying at them. The two men
duck, then straighten, looking in. Ermanno, with whisky
bottle in hand, he grabs at some whore in the tavern
wanting to force himself onto her. "Ermanno!" Koza yells.
The few other men, a mix of soldiers and servants look
back to Ermanno. The man lets go of the woman who is
quick to get away. "What the hell do you think you are
doing?!"

The indignant Second Lieutenant walks toward his
comrades. "Oh come on, Koza! You do not think Eber
meant his orders, do you?!" Ermanno booms in Koza's
face.

Koza glances around the room. "You know the
Commander always means his orders, idiot!" he looks to
the bottle. "How much have you drunk?"

Thayer speaks his mind quietly, "General Soldat is
right," he leans toward Ermanno. "We do not know what
of our previous behavior we can partake in, how do you
know what that drink will do to you?"

Defiantly, Ermanno claims, "It will do nothing!" He
swigs a gulp from the bottle. "See!" Suddenly, he heaves
his body at one of the merchants sitting at a table in the
tavern and spews everything he has eaten in a month onto
the floor in front of the man, almost on his shoes.
Everyone cringes at the colorful and chunky sight. The
man climbs from the table and runs screaming.

From behind Koza and Thayer comes, "That is why I
told you not to drink anything." The two men jump and
move aside for their commander.

Eber steps up to Ermanno who takes a second and looks
up. "Hello." Ermanno smiles up at Eber who stares down

coldly at him. Then the Commander raises his foot, and with full force smashes Ermanno's face down into the spew on the floor. Everyone cringes even more. Ermanno flails his arms and legs getting nowhere.

Eber looks back at Koza and Thayer, "The three of you will go to my house and stay there. When I get there, if I find one of you missing… I will kill all of you." He takes his boot from the back of Ermanno's bald head, letting him breathe again. When Eber reaches the entry to the tavern, he adds, "And Ermanno, do not bring one bit of that in through my door." Ermanno looks up at his comrades with a layer of spew on his face.

KAPITEL V

Bibi – Of Romani origin. Described as a tall, thin, barefoot woman dressed in red. Some gypsies tell of seeing two lambs by her side, their gentle blood feeding her, while others say they are children whose souls now belong to her. The bargains of fate in which she deals often trade mortals their greedy, twisted and dangerous desires for something of value to only her, be it fancy garments, a single hair from their head, or whatever else she may need for her dark workings. The men and women who go to the Bibi are of the most desperate for what they want for the Devil himself can write no better contract than she.

Outside of the city's southeast fortress walls, near the river that flows from the north, through a bulk of the city and around the south mountains, lies a camp. A small society of wagons and tents sets nestled amongst the forest. Gypsies, Romani people, are completely unto themselves. Though the sophisticated people of Loviturä consider themselves high above common gypsies, the populace of Loviturä has not insisted they be run off. Instead, annual festivities welcome the gypsies as suppliers of much of the entertainment, but despite this form of acceptance, the Romani people here would never regard themselves as civilians of Loviturä.

There are many bonfires tonight as it is a cold night. One fire situated between three wagons supplies warmth to several gypsies. Men and women talk as children chase one another in their young games. Of a sudden, one of the men grows silent and soon another. As the quietness spreads through them, each gypsy turns the way of the first, looking for what is causing this disruption.

Like a shadow through the trees, Eber moves at the edge of the camp, destined for something farther in the woods. His passing, holds the attentions of many, but the eyes that linger on him long after the men and women go back to their talking, are those of the tribe leader. Elder Azzo watches Eber, the soldier not a complete stranger to him.

Deeper in the woods, there sets a vardo wagon, and next to it, a bender tent of good size. Within the bender tent, there is a colorful home. Glass bottles of varied size, shape, hue rest on small tables and hang from the wooden framework of the tent. Finely carved non-matching furniture pieces make places for conversation and relaxation, setting atop large rugs that spread over the dirt floors, covering the ground in patterns and colors.

The center of the tent is a huge fire pit, alight with burning logs, smoke rising up and out of the open flaps in the roof of the tent. And at that center, around that fire, sits a middle-aged woman. Her long black hair drapes over her shoulder, her black lashes encircling bright blue eyes that watch the fire like glowing orbs. Her clothes are simple, two layers of skirts bound to her waist by ties and an underbust corset. The sleeves of a man's shirt, much like that of a soldier's uniform, hang down her arms, past her hands. Over top it all, her shoulders stay warm under a bright red shawl.

Peacefully, she pokes at the fire with a rod, sparking new flames on the wood when gradually there is a chill the fire can not warm. Drifting her gaze, she slowly looks from the fire over her shoulder, finding Eber near her, watching. She jumps to her bare feet. "A Der Vorfahr soldier?" She sets the back of her slim hand to her forehead. "Have you come to hurt me?" Her eyes cast his way, fluttering her black lashes. "Or have you come to defile me?" She grows a smirk. "I really hope it's the second one." With that, the damsel act is gone.

"Lorelei," he says tolerantly.

"Oooh, you said my name, this must be important." She muses, crossing her arms.

"Perhaps." He ventures near one of her tables at the edge of the tent's curved walls. "It is not exaggeration to say I need you."

"Need me? The mighty soldier named, Soldier? Whatever for?" She watches him peruse her items on the table. Finding a necklace adorned by a small silver cross, he lifts the chain, drawing the cross into his palm. Tilting her head, her brow wrinkles at his actions when there is a sound like tinder on a fire, the hissing noise of something burning. She looks back down to his hand and sees the cross beginning to burn him. At once, her play and toying fades, her face showing something genuine instead as she rushes toward him. Snatching the cross from his palm, she tosses the necklace to the side, holding his palm up for her to see. The cross's shape is seared into his skin, the burns looking unbearable. "Eber," her low voice says under her breath. Moving from him, she collects a cloth and dunks it in a small barrel of cool water, returning to him. "Tell me what happened." He observes her ask whilst she wraps his hand. Watching her, her wavy hair bunches over her shoulder, brushing against her face with her arm's movements, those blue eyes glancing up rarely to peer into his soul. Steadily, Eber feels the familiar sharp pain in his chest he ignores.

His manner shifts back to its lifelessness. "I was killed in battle… Battle against my own… Men I had watched die came back from the dead. They killed all of us who were left. I and three of my army awakened from our deaths and have returned to Loviturä."

Hearing his story, her study of his face lingers in his dark eyes. "How is that possible?" She says more to herself.

"I would expect you to have that answer."

Flustered, she spouts, "I am the one who did this to you, Soldier." She pokes at his chest. "But even I do not know every facet to it." Glaring at him, his calmness begins to quiet her. Finally, she shrugs. "I guess you should just count your blessings." She pauses and stares at him as he does the same down on her. "Get it?" She pokes her elbow into his side. "Because you are damned." Her heavy brows lift. His stare holds. Her brows lower with her lips. "You were more fun before you died… sort of." She rolls her eyes, her body turning with them. "You said you need me. What for?"

His gaze follows her. "I want guidance."

"Guidance?"

"In one day I will be leading an escort to the village of Hieb, nothing must go wrong and yet I know little about what I now am, that is not good. I need to know what hunger I may expect, what urges. I need the guidance of one with more knowledge than I have with the matter at hand."

"Whom are you escorting?"

He pauses. "Ambrozij Kasimir."

A grin grows on the woman's face and she begins to laugh. "An untoter guarding the Head of the Church!" She collects herself and looks him over. "Now, you have to find that funny."

"...There is an irony to it." He stares dully. "As I said, Lorelei, I need you."

The play to her blue orbs fades into the warmth also in them, her air becoming more serious as her tone shows a touch of devotion. "You have me."

After sending Thayer to acquire fresh clothes from their usual barracks, his young friend returned with the clean garments.

Koza sits in a tall backed chair next to the fireplace in the living room of Eber's home whilst Ermanno lies on the couch opposite him. Finding his own comfort atop one of the chair's stool, Thayer passes his gaze over the walls of the home.

This house of Eber's is its own sort of castle with grandiose rooms and high ceilings. The walls are lined with detailed frescos of reds, gold, deep browns and black. If one stared long enough at the patterns on the walls made by those colors, steadily, images appear as faces with eyes looking back at you. The fine furniture reflects the beauty and polish of the manor house with expensive rugs dotting the wooden floors throughout.

The outside is as looming and dark as the inside. The house is set on a low cliff that connects to the waterfront of the wide river below, which gives a view of the city's harbor down the way.

The house was given to Eber by Berin for deeds well done, a few of those rewarded deeds meant to stay tightly behind Eber's lips.

Koza leans forward, his elbows setting to his knees and hands rubbing together as he stares into the flames of the fire in the large stone fireplace, sculptures of dragons rising from the mantle with roaring open mouths. Anxious, he says to himself, "I wonder where the Commander went?"

"Maybe he went to speak with family?" Thayer proposes, his seat on a stool near Koza's chair.

"You think Eber has family?" Ermanno spouts at leisure while lying on the couch with his eyes closed and arms behind his head.

"Does not everyone?" young Thayer asks from his stool.

"Brigadier General Eber Soldat's body was forged like a sword in the fires of Hell." The two men look to Ermanno who rolls his head and opens his eyes, growing a toothy grin at them. "But that is just my opinion."

Softly, a knock comes to the front door of the house, drawing all to turn.

Rising to his feet, Koza moves for the door, pausing before opening it wide. Lorelei stands with hands holding a large bag in front of her. "Who are you?"

"A friend," she smiles innocently.

Taken aback by the pleasant expression on her already attractive face, Koza gawks. "Uh, friend?" She steps past him and moves inside. "The Commander has friends?" He trails her.

Her innocent smile turns to more of a devilish smirk. "Surprising, is it not?"

Gathering his manners, Koza leans. "Uh, what is your name, Madam?"

"Lorelei. Lorelei Zima," she answers, her bright blue eyes casting up to him under her dark lashes. "You?"

He sets a hand to his chest and gives a little bow. "My name is Mikhail Koza." The fashion of his uniform adding the title of Captain to his name, her eyes recognizing the clothes from the years she saw Eber in them. "That is Johan Thayer." He aims a hand towards the young man with messy blond locks. "And that is Adolpho Ermanno." Koza cringes at the somewhat psychotic smirk that crawls up Ermanno's cheek at the woman.

"And how can we be certain you are a friend of the Commander, and not one of his many enemies who is worming her way into his home?" Ermanno sets his knees into Koza's empty chair, hanging past the high back. "Hm?" That innocence returns to her smile as she reaches into a pouch hanging from the waist of her corset, and pulls out a very small amount of some kind of powder. She then blows it with a little puff into the man's face.

"Aaahhh! It burns! Why is it burning?!" His hands slap over his eyes and he falls onto the floor, flopping around in pain.

She watches him writhe with no sympathy as Koza and Thayer flinch and get closer to one another. "It is garlic, dried and ground into a fine powder. It will stop hurting when it burns away… eventually." Lorelei waves a hand over Ermanno and his yelps. "Those screams are enough to wake the dead." Koza and Thayer look to her as she chuckles. "What am I saying? You are already dead." She pokes Koza in the ribs with an elbow, ending her laugh with a snort.

"I see you are acquainting yourself with everyone," Eber says from behind the group.

Koza and Thayer release a couple of tenor screams of surprise. Turning casually, Lorelei looks him up and down unenthusiastically. "Commander, do you know this woman?" Koza asks.

"The Gypsy is here to assist us in learning more about what we now are."

"I see."

"What is the first step?" Thayer queries.

Regaining his wits, Ermanno creeps to his feet, his eyes watering. She sets her bag on a small table against the wall and rummages through it. "I suppose we should first begin with learning just what kind of undead each of you are."

Thayer speaks again, "What do you mean what kind of undead we are?"

She pulls her hands out of her bag and rests them on the stiff mouth of it by the handles. "Well…" she cocks her head and looks up at the ceiling, then turns to Thayer. "You see, there are literally countless chronicles of the undead." She steps up to Thayer. "There are tales of creatures which feed on blood." She peruses the faces of the men, passing them a soothsayer gleam in her eyes. "Some have been known to feed on the bodies of their fellow departed… There are even some who are said to only feed on energy," she stops in front of Eber and meets his gaze. "Such as… sexual energy." She pauses and arches a thick eyebrow. "What are you hungry for, Soldier?" Lorelei teases with a grin and holds her stare on him. He doesn't blink, thoroughly acquainted with the Gypsy's humor.

"Excuse me?" Thayer interrupts the moment. The Commander and the Gypsy turn their heads faintly to look at the young man. "I am not hungry for anything. What does that mean?"

An immediate thought strikes Lorelei. "Have you not undergone rigor mortis yet?"

Confused, Thayer asks, "Rigor mortis?"

Eber answers the question, still in his tepid posture. "Rigor mortis is a term used when a body becomes stiff after death." He turns back to the Gypsy. "I do not understand the connection? We are not the dead, we are the undead."

"Which is why rigor mortis for you has a different meaning." She looks to the group. "For you, it is something that earmarks a progression in what you now are."

"It is a change we will all go through?"

"You must remember Eber, legend is not science. I know more fables than facts." She gives him a cold stare which he returns. "I would imagine it to be quite painful. Perhaps, the science of it is that bones are becoming stronger or the skin is developing a restorative aspect. Whatever the reason for its happening, I believe that this stage of existence for untoten is what makes them the monsters that they are."

Ermanno says with delight, "Wonderful, so we have more pain to look forward to."

Koza crosses his arms and turns to the axe wielding, run head long into violent battle, years since having a sane thought man and rebuttals, "I think perhaps you have already experienced it."

"Why do you say that?" Lorelei asks.

"When we were still at the battlefield, after Ermanno returned from the dead, he wanted to eat the dead bodies of our fellow soldiers."

Lorelei allocates the bald man a leery eye, as do Koza and Thayer in reminiscing the event. Ermanno gives the room a deviant look. "I did not undergo rigor mortis, wanting to eat a dead man was simply a whim."

"You have a sick mind, Ermanno." Koza looks to the floor and shakes his head.

"Gypsy," she turns up to Eber. "Are you still able to distinguish what sort of Undead we are without having undergone rigor mortis?"

She smirks. "To an extent, but keep in mind many are individual even among their own types of Untoten." She steps to Ermanno. "Where are you from?"

"Italy."

She slaps him on his bald head. "You think I do not know your accent you idiot! What part of Italy?" her own Slavic accent thick and deep.

"Violenza," he sneers.

She clasps her hands together behind her back and 'hmms' with interest. "In that region of Italy most undead are depicted as Lemures."

"And what are they?" Koza speaks.

"They are unsettled, nomadic dead that are known to be vengeful at times. They are violent and vicious Di Inferi," she peeks back at Koza from over her shoulder. "They are called, gods of the underworld."

Ermanno grins, every tooth in his head having become pointier since awakening from his death, but no less crooked. "I like how that sounds."

Lorelei turns a look back to him with more wisdom and malevolence behind her grin. "Do you?"

The man raises his eyebrows. "Shouldn't I?"

Her lips curl on one side as she moves on to Thayer. "And what of you? What village or city are you from?"

"Pochva, Muscovy." He shields his head in a quick motion.

She arches a brow. "Well, since you were not revived from the dead by sorcery you are not an Eretica." She puts a slim finger to her pink lips. "I am sorry young one, I am not certain of your species." Then, she walks to Koza. "You?"

"Johan Thayer and I are from the same town."

She scrolls a pondering stare over his body, then back up to his eyes. "You are the most human looking of the group… you puzzle me." She turns from him and moves toward Eber. "You are not as obvious as your Commander."

"Obvious?" Eber's voice deepens.

"Quite." The Gypsy walks to his front and gazes up to his black heartless eyes. "A man as strong as you are, cruel as you are, having come from the north of the country could be only one creature, a Nachzehrer." He stares down at her unaffected by the claim.

The Gypsy goes to her bag and pulls out a wine bottle. The label is shredded and visibly quite old. She heads off into the direction of the kitchen and a moment later comes back with three glasses. "She knows where the kitchen is?" Koza leans to his comrades becoming more curious about her familiarity with the Commander.

Biting the cork, she pops it out of the bottle with her teeth and pours a clear liquid. She walks to each man handing them a glass with the exception being Eber. The men look warily at the drinks and each other. "This is liquor?" Ermanno asks with high hopes.

"It will have a burn like liquor." Eber suspiciously watches the Gypsy not really ever able to guess what she is going to do.

Ermanno accepts what Lorelei says without any thought and drinks down the liquid in one swallow. Koza reacts, "Ermanno!" thinking what a fool the man is.

"It tastes fine to me!" Koza and Thayer pass looks of caution and trepidation to each other. "It doesn't taste like alcohol though?" Ermanno peers closer at his empty glass while smacking his lips. Lorelei stands in front of Ermanno watching him as Eber stands several centimeters behind her doing the same thing.

Immediately, something begins to happen and Ermanno's movements start becoming pained. He grabs his throat and all but a fire roars out when he opens his mouth and yells. Ermanno tears past Lorelei and Eber out to the balcony, down steps that wined through hillside vegetation to the river's edge and dunks his head into the cool relief. Back in the house, Lorelei turns to the men. "What are you waiting for? Drink up." They look to her in horror.

Ermanno comes back up into the house looking like Hell. "What was that?!" his eyes dead set on the Gypsy.

Her voice is eased. "Holy Water."

Koza and Thayer glare down at their glasses. "Holy Water?! You had me drink Holy Water?!"

"You seemed quite happy to."

His eyes flare a golden anger that becomes brighter the closer he gets to her. "You tricked me Gypsy whore!" With every step closer he takes, she takes no step back. She stands unaffected by his aggression. Just as Ermanno reaches Lorelei, Her bright blue eyes begin to glow. Halting, Ermanno nearly jumps back in fear of what it means. He gawks as she slides her lips into her cheeks, her blue orbs dulling with Ermanno's cowardice retreat from her.

"...I am not one to be threatened, soldier." Where her manner had been playful, the tone to her low voice changes and with a subtlety, she warns. "Do not entice this cat to take a bite of the mouse she plays with." She moves along to Koza and Thayer from Ermanno as if he had been an immaterial danger. "Now for the both of you." They are reluctant. "Drink," she commands. The men drink.

A tiny sip each then Thayer cries, "It hurts. God! Ah! It hurt to say God! Ah! I said it again!" He all but drops to the floor.

Koza stands with his eyes shut hard, waiting for the expected pain yet receives nothing. His breathing is hastened by one expectation of harm after the other. He cracks one eye open then the other, then his body loosens its tension and the strong, youthful muscles relax under his shirt and short-waisted army coat.

Lorelei steps up to him and stares. He holds his head back fearful of what she may be up to now. "Interesting? You can be drenched with holy water, wear a cross, touch the robe of a priest and feel nothing." She turns to Eber with a smile. "That will be useful." Eber holds his gaze on her then on Koza, silently judging her words. She walks from Koza to the side of the Commander. "So!" With a slow blink, Eber's eyes go from Koza to her. "Now for the next part in this evening's self-awareness lessons." She grins and gives the Commander a sideways gleam.

KAPITEL VIII

Outside Loviturä, the soldiers climb a hillside, accompanied by the Gypsy. "So, why are we here?" The bright moon lights the land.

As Lorelei begins to respond to Koza's question, "Because-"

"We must learn how the changes to our bodies affect our fighting." Eber steals the answer as he passes by her continuing up the hill.

"Yes." She frowns her eyebrows that he interrupted her and picks up her pace to get ahead of him once more. They reach the top and settle for a flat section of land.

"And how are we going to learn about these changes?" Koza asks as he surveys the surroundings.

She takes a stance in front of the men. "Simple... fight for your lives." The night shifts, as if something controls it. The trees grow darker and slowly this feeling of despair spreads like a low fog across the ground. "Before you died you were soldiers of the King, now you are predators of the Devil."

The moon begins to shine brighter in this place of increasing darkness, stretching the shadows of the men. Koza watches the woman as her blue eyes start to match the brightness of the moon above. Suddenly, Koza's stretching shadow begins to move, to twist and coil on the grassy dirt. It is no longer the flat image of the soldier. The thing rises from the ground and draws the reflecting image of Koza's sword. The soldier stands agape at the sight. Ermanno and Thayer look on in amazement, while Eber seems to have seen this trick before. The shadow swipes at

Koza who ducks out of reflex. He swears he could feel the air rush by him from the swipe.

The shadow lunges for him and he jumps back, avoiding contact with its blade, his blade, "If this thing is real enough to strike, then surely it is real enough to be killed, but is it possible to kill a shadow?" his mind races with other worldly questions and presumed answers. Finally, the shadow strikes a tree cutting a limb clean off. Koza watches the limb fall in front of him and he looks up in shock at the wavy image he can't escape.

Koza closes his eyes and waits as the shadow draws back for another swing, then just as it moves to attack, it bows back to the ground at his feet and becomes a part of him again. "I am not impressed," the woman picks at him, having had to call the creature off to spare him. Koza passes his shaky gaze to Eber and can see the man is thinking the same thing of him. He drops his eyes to the ground at his shadow as he breathes heavily, regaining his composure.

Ermanno chuckles drawing all to look at him. "You may have creepy shadows, but you're still just a woman. Let me show you what I can do." He pulls the large battle axe from his back and runs at her screaming. His enthusiasm is unmatched as he rushes her. But just as he reaches her and draws back with the deadly weapon, she yanks a colorful bandana from her mess of clothes and as if it takes a life of its own wraps itself around Ermanno's head. He swings the axe and misses now being unable to see. With a light poke, she sends him rolling and yelling down the hill they had all labored to climb.

After an enjoyable pause, watching the crazy bald man, she turns to the youngest. Thayer meets her gaze and she asks, "And you young one?"

Thayer stutters his answer, "If Koza didn't stand a chance then neither do I."

To justify his young friend's fear, Koza speaks up, "We have never known anything like you. You are another level of battle."

She stares at him blandly. "A level you now stand on with me." Koza and Thayer pay heed to her words knowing she has wisdom of things that to them were only fables. "Widen your eyes soldiers, your time of human wars has passed." Ermanno finally reaches the top of the hill having ripped apart the bandana, leaving shreds of it on his clothing. "Spend the night fighting amongst yourselves if need be for the importance of learning what you can now do, is immeasurable."

A short time passes and Eber stands at the treeline with his arms folded, while watching the familiar sight of his men practicing. Little by little one of them discovers another inhuman trait and works to hone it. They begin to move away from the necessity of their weapons, finding otherworldly strength and speed, even hearing and smell to aid them as well as a sharp blade or arrow. The skill Ermanno appears to favor is his new capability to appease his savagery to its fullest. Ermanno gives an animal yell and lunges for Thayer who chooses to run. "The bald man is insane," Lorelei comments sitting on a rounded stone by Eber.

"Each one of them possesses something useful to me," he replies drably.

She turns her gaze up to him with a smirk. "Tell me."

"Thayer is a mother's son. He is a cowered in hand to hand combat, but left to himself in a place that offers stealth, he is the best shot with a bow and arrow I have ever seen."

She toys with a lackluster finger on her lip. "To impress you is impressive." She smirks. "And the crazy one?"

The scene of Ermanno chasing Thayer with a smile of crooked pointy teeth spread on his face and Koza trying to bring a stop to it. Eber drops his gaze down to her. "He is… eager."

Lorelei studies Koza closely. "Koza is special now, but what made him so in life?"

The commander watches his young Captain. "Loyalty."

"Feel you can turn your back on him do you?" she smirks sideways up to him.

"He's the only one." Eber reconsiders his thoughts and turns his expressionless gaze down at her. "Other than you." It is a statement said coldly, but suggests a warmth that existed at one time, a time Lorelei's gaze lowers to the ground in thought of.

"Commander!" Koza calls as he approaches. "I believe Ermanno is undergoing rigor mortis."

They turn their attention outward and see Ermanno convulsing on the ground. He thrashes like a man more wild than usual. Thayer is attempting to single-handedly hold him down as Koza rushes to help his friend in the task. Hurriedly, the Gypsy grabs one of the sticks which the forest has plentifully provided on the ground. She kneels beside the thrashing bald man and commands Koza to open the man's mouth. Koza grabs Ermanno's gnashing jaw. "Take care he does not bite off your fingers!" the Gypsy orders in a high voice to try and overtake Ermanno's booming yells of muscle twisting pain. Koza pulls at Ermanno's jaw, opening his mouth as Lorelei braces the stick between his teeth. Eber stands, watching over the scene. Of a sudden, Thayer heaves backwards and begins the same convulsions as Ermanno. The man being younger than even Koza, his screams are higher pitched than Ermanno and even the more indicating of great pain. The woman tells Koza to focus on Ermanno while she tasks herself with the smaller man.

An hour or so later, Koza, Thayer and Ermanno rest themselves on the dirt, having each undergone their own torture of rigor mortis, not even after they had been killed on the battlefield have they looked so dead. Lorelei sits resting on a downed tree while Eber sits beside her. Aware of all their eyes as they stare at him merely waiting, wondering when the Commander would be next to writhe. "Stop staring at me." His voice is low and not accepting of their glares.

The Gypsy leads the turn of all their heads to look elsewhere. After perusing her gaze over the tattered men, she gets to her feet in a huff of breath. "Well!" All eyes go to her. "I am sure your muscles feel abusively strained." A collective groan comes from the lot. "Come!" she says sharply and begins to head back towards Loviturä.

Koza stretches the tendons in his neck to watch her. "What now?!" he shouts to the woman leaving them behind.

She turns and with a less mischievous grin than usual says, "Sweet relief."

KAPITEL IX

With the night as a thick ebony haze, they easily tread through the Romani camp. Glowing lanterns hang from the gypsy wagons and sway in the cool breeze. Still burning fires entice gatherings of fellow gypsies to the warmth. They trade stories and jokes as Lorelei and the soldiers pass through the outskirts of the camp, but still close enough to hear every word and roaring laugh that escapes the heavy bellies of some of the elders.

They reach her wagon and tent through the woods, beyond the mild clearing that resides the rest of her tribe. Entering her bender tent, she strikes a match to a dim lamp. Looking over the tent, Koza pans her room of knick knacks, seeing a life of magic in the colorful potions in bottles, hanging and setting on tables.

Gradually, each man finds a spot he makes his own. Thayer drops by the fire at the center of the tent, while Ermanno flops to one of the rugs. Koza strides casually by the random items of the Gypsy, looking over everything, from furs and books, to bones that rest in sorted arrangement on a table.

With comfort seeming to be on his mind, Eber aims for the woman's bed in the back of the tent, curtained by heavily embroidered drapes with golden tassels tied back. It is a nest of sorted pillows strewn about with the covers tossed to the side. Watching Eber, Koza notes his familiarity with this place and with the woman. All of it is odd to Koza. Much as he has learned of the Commander over time, he would never have assumed he had such allies as this woman, if ally is what he calls her, and not more.

The Gypsy grabs a thin bottle from a shelf and plunks it on a table. "This is a liquid that will help your muscles relax. It will make you feel better."

Ermanno grabs for it needing no more encouragement to want it and begins to drain the bottle. Thayer pulls it from his hand and consumes his own portion. Thayer lowers the bottle from his lips and a panicked look streaks across his face as in a flash he runs from the tent, when he reaches outside, he can hold back no longer and a violent spew comes burning up his throat from his stomach.

"Poor child." Ermanno throws a thumb over his shoulder musing about the lad's Hell. Just that moment, Ermanno's lips purse and his cheeks bloat, and in a single leap, he overtakes Thayer's poison at the entrance hurling his own wicked concoction.

"That is my front door," she grumbles.

"I will insure they clean it up." Koza turns to her.

"Your self-control will always be an asset to you. Always remember that, Captain." She hands him the bottle. "This was not meant to be swallowed. Instead, it is a combination of rubbing oils and minerals. It is meant for living men, but muscles are muscles." He takes a single drop from the vile and in a moment of dreading anticipation, he begins to rub the clear oil onto his forearm.

A wave of relief washes over him as the ointment does not hurt, but help. "It is remarkable." He gives an appeased smile. "It is already working." He sets down the bottle and begins to unbutton his crisp white shirt, but then he hesitates and looks to the woman. "May I remove my shirt in your presence?"

She grins and leans her chin into her palms, setting her elbows to the table. "Please do." She bites on a finger.

Blinking, he gives a subtle nod and begins to unclothe his lengthy torso, pulling his shirt tails from the waist of his slender black uniform breeches. He finishes unbuttoning the shirt and slides it off his round shoulders.

Lorelei's gaze follows the descent of the shirt but stays on his body as he tosses it to a nearby chair. Her lips part and her eyes roam. His skin is tan in shade, still the color of a healthy living man.

Just as he is about to put another lending of the lotion to himself, she springs from her place at the table and comes to his aid. "Let me help you!" She stands before him eager to have at it. "I am the one who made the lotion, therefore, I am the one who best knows how to… rub it on." She bats her dark long lashes.

"Uh, I suppose."

She dumps a gob in her hand and starts to spread it over his chest matting the light furring of it to his skin. "Yeees, this will help those muscles… Those very large muscles." She beams in her own world of delight.

Without opening an eye, Eber asks while lying comfortably on the bed, "Have care Koza, else she will steal your innocence." He looks back to Lorelei.

"Go back to sleep," she hisses.

Back to her work, Lorelei massages the oil over Koza and rubs it across his arm. Taking the odd chance this moment presents to him, he glances to Eber to see the man's reaction. Eber toys with her, but does the Commander truly care about this woman touching another man? The Gypsy plays that she could be more to him than an ally, yet perhaps play is all it is. Eber lies undisturbed by her actions. He does not act a jealous man if this woman were his.

Suddenly, Eber opens his eyes with a hint of a scowl and rises from the bed. Koza and the woman look on at him in wonder of the shift in demeanor. "I don't hear Ermanno and Thayer anymore." Koza perks, now aware of the same. Grabbing his shirt, Koza moves outside to find them indeed, gone.

Eber and Lorelei move to the door, and at that moment, the high pitched cry of a young child sounds in the distance, near the tribe of gypsies. In the vibration of air that is becoming nearly routine for him, Eber is gone, becoming but a memory beside Lorelei.

KAPITEL X

Upyr – Of Muscovian origin. Claimed to be one of the most vicious of the Muscovian undead, the Upyr is a creature that walks during the day and sleeps at night, though some legends tell of the beast not sleeping at all. It has a definite taste for blood, but prefers it to be of a younger age. It tends to eat only children, but has been found munching on their grieving parents.

A small girl runs under a wagon on the outskirts of the camp. She tries to seek refuge beneath the wagon behind one of its wheels. She lets out a cry and huddles her face into her arms on the ground when she sees Ermanno fling himself onto the dirt before the wagon. Frantically, he tries to crawl underneath to bury his teeth into the child. Whatever mind the crazy bald man had, is gone completely, now there is but pure unwavering hunger.

Just as Ermanno can barely reach her, his leg is seized by the iron grip of the Commander, and his body is hurled back out from under the wagon and thrown nearly into the treeline a good deal away. On the other side of the wagon, Thayer is making his attempt at the child when his shoulders are taken and roughly shook by Koza.

"What are you doing?! Stop this!" The violent jarring Koza gives his friend brings him into awareness. Just as Lorelei arrives, she sees Ermanno rise to his feet still in a state of enraged hunger. He rushes Eber appearing as a rabid animal bent on a kill. Being a hard man to threaten, Eber draws no blade nor does he even seem to prepare himself for the attack. Stumbling to his feet, Ermanno shakes his head and narrows his eyes on the Commander. A snarl creeps across his face as he bares his fangs at Eber. Lowly, a growl rolls up Eber's throat. At once, the feral Ermanno responds like the animal he is becoming, jerking his head and lowering his gaze from the cold one of Eber's.

In the fray, the girl scrambles from the wagon and makes for an escape to tell all what she has seen. "Wait!" Koza calls. Eber shifts through the shadows again, appearing beside the child and snatching her up in one of his arms. The girl screams and Eber muffles her cries, holding her at a cockeyed angle whilst she fights. "What are we going to do with her?" Koza asks frantically, fearing he knows the answer. Quietly, Lorelei comes to the scene from the shadows, listening to Koza.

Eber turns and begins to walk with the girl thrashing in his arm. "I will drown her in the river, it will be a believable death for a child."

Koza's eyes flare with desperate plea as he runs to cut his Commander off. "No!"

"No?" Again, a growl rumbles from the Commander at the younger male presenting him a challenge of authority.

Knowing an outright demand of the Commander is not the best of ideas, he bows his head and loosens his tense body in complete submission. "Please, please, I beg of you, not a child."

With no change in his expression, Eber steps past Koza having no intention of stopping. Koza stares at the ground as he thinks of something which makes his breathing strain. He slowly moves his hand to the grip of his sword, his hand trembles slightly at the idea of challenging his Commander.

Passing by Lorelei, She breathes to him, "Eber." He stops. Eber heeds as she gradually lifts her hand between them, gently grasping the hilt of his sword at his side. "Not a child." Her tone is unlike any other time. Her words said softly up to him. Slowly, in Koza's mind, he begins to swear he can hear a faint hum, as though metal was vibrating. The more he listens, the more he realizes the hum is coming from Eber's sword. Seeming to come out of a haze, Eber's eyes gain life to them. It is a life that is accompanied by that pain in his chest. He looks to the child in his arm and begins to lower her to the ground as if not remembering picking her up.

Koza's hand slides off his sword as he tries to understand what he is seeing. Soft words from her and Eber obeys. Lorelei's hand slips off Eber's sword and once more, his eyes are cold and lifeless.

"Lulu! Lulu!"

The unfamiliar holler comes up on them quickly, only giving time for Lorelei to say, "Get into the shadows." Koza, Thayer and Ermanno abide and she grabs the girl, heaving her at the group of men just coming into sight. The men halt as they see Lorelei standing beside the familiar soldier.

The obvious father of the girl rushes to her, swooping her up close to him. "I have told you to stay away from the Bibi! Never go near her!"

Lorelei steps away from Eber who did not run to the shadows. "For their safety, I have warned all of you to keep your curious children away from my affairs." Her voice is deep and looming.

"Papa! There were monsters. They wanted to eat me!" the girl sobs in her father's arms.

With refined poise, Lorelei retorts, "What other than monsters do you think I would have for pets?" She takes the brunt of accusations so that no one might go looking for other answers to the girl's cries.

"We should not stand for your witchery!" one man dares step forward and speak up. "You should be hung by the neck until your body swings limp!" There is but a murmur of agreement from the group behind him.

Casually, the elder leader comes through the group to the front. Azzo examines Lorelei, then moves his gaze to Eber. "You forget the good she has done for us." He looks back at her. "…I do not." Having enough of the excitement, the tribe leader turns. "Come, let us go back to our own business." The men trail along, unhappy to dismiss the woman over past favors like Azzo.

Thayer comes from the shadows, watching the people leave and taking in a deep breath. "I am sorry Commander." He attempts to regain his place in the ranks. "When I saw Ermanno go for the girl I followed, it was a hunger like never before."

"Is that not what the Gypsy warned?" Eber replies unsympathetically.

Thayer shifts his glance to the woman. "Yes Sir."

"Then you should have been prepared."

"Yes Sir."

The Gypsy crosses her arms and swings a glare at the young man. "Well, at least now I know you are a Upyr sort of untoten." The men look at her having no clue what that means. She scrutinizes their faces. "It is an Undead that favors the taste of children." Thayer lowers his head again as his comrades look back at him.

"Commander, permission to speak?" Eber turns a look to Koza. "We all hunger now, even I am starving. It will take every bit of willpower to not show that hunger in front of Kasimir… What are we going to do?"

Interrupting the moment of silent thought, Lorelei speaks up, "There are always the prisons." She arches a heavy brow. "Deep in the bowels of Reinhard Castle, there are captives long forgotten, guarded by no one. And the best part is that the cells are enclosed by thick stone buried in the earth where no pleas for mercy or cries for help can be heard." Koza gapes at the woman, seeing the viciousness of her sharp mind. She is survival at its most wise and beautiful.

"Koza." Koza snaps from his thoughts and turns to Eber. "You will take Thayer and Ermanno to the deepest cells in the castle and satiate your hungers, being sure to not leave a hint of what killed the prisoners, understand?"

"Yes Sir." He shifts his eyes not wanting the task. "But Sir, I do not hunger for blood."

"What do you hunger for then?" Eber truly wonders.

Koza averts his glances to the others not quite knowing how to say it. "I am hungry… for… fish."

"Fish?" Eber remarks followed by Thayer and Ermanno, then Lorelei.

"That is what the Upir eats as he does not feed on blood, instead he consumes fish. Yet another mock of humanity which may prove this man useful to you, Soldier." She grins at the General.

Eber looks back to Koza. "Then find your fill wherever you wish, but you will still carryout my orders."

"Yes Sir." He nods reluctantly.

In the dark of the dungeon, there is a single row of lights lining the wide stone hall. Koza opens the large door which in turn makes a deafening grind, the hinges have given to rust from lack of use, say for the occasional meal being brought to the prisoners. In a sick twist of irony, no meal is being brought by these soldiers for that is what the prisoners are intended to be to them. As the door sounds, rustling comes from the line of cells and hands reach out between the bars.

Koza stops, not wanting to see the faces of the few prisoners. He takes the key from the hook on the wall and hands it to Thayer beside him. Not a word is exchanged as the key drops to Thayer's waiting hand, only regret and hesitation are remarked by Koza's richly green eyes. As Thayer leaves him, Ermanno steps up and slaps a chipped plate on the small slanted table that rests under the key hook.

"Koza, look." Koza passes a glance at the remains on the plate and then to Ermanno. "It must have been the lunch of a guard, fish." The bald man grins widely, then joins Thayer's approach to the first cell in the row which is housing the few captives as Koza watches.

Though his eyes are open Koza's mind fades, leaving him only the sense of hearing. The shuffle of prisoners backing from the door not knowing what to expect, the key turning the workings of the lock, the cell door swinging open with heavy creaks, the snarls and guttural growls as the hunger again takes rein of the two soldiers, the screaming that starts and desperate cries for help. His sight comes back to him as he looks down to the plate of old fish, not feeling hungry anymore.

The late hours creep as the earth seems to relish the night, bidding it to stay. The moonlight ripples on the flowing water of the Ita River as its current gentles in a small alcove. As you trail your gaze in the alcove from its water, to its sandy edge and up the steep hillside covered in lush foliage, spotted with trees and indented by a winding path of steps and landings, you see at the top the cold stones of Eber's grand house.

Though it is cold on the outside there is warmth on the inside, the warmth being from Lorelei's bath of hot water. She rests in the claw-footed tub in the bath of the master bedroom. Her hair is tied up into a mess and one leg sets out of the bubbled water on the tub's rim.

"Even after all this time, I am still not accustomed to the idea of hot water from a pipe." Raising her hand from the bath she taps the faucet with a finger while contemplating the workings of it.

Compared to the Roman Empire, Loviturä has made itself known for advances in civility, enticing the wealthy and powerful to take residence in the city. It supplies luxuries such as clothing markets, large stores where the finest fabrics are already made and so varied that any size wearer can be accommodated. There is dining of highest quality and class, using foods of rare tastes. Yet another marvel being its inventions of comfort, like the tapping of underground hot springs beneath the city to flow from the faucets of homes.

After drying off, she slips the layer of white shirt up her shoulders, loosely buttoning it down her front. Stepping out from the bathroom, Lorelei stops at the edge of the bed, casually staring down at Eber. He rests atop the covers in a position of contentment, fingers of both hands interlocked on his stomach and eyes gently closed. His sword sets upright leaning against the side of the bed an easy reach away. His heavy uniform coat has been shed and thrown over a chair in the room, along with the black leather jerkin and tall boots carelessly dropped on the floor.

Reaching up to her mess of wavy hair, Lorelei untangles braids as she reflects on the evening. "Ever growing in threat are you not, Soldier?" She smiles, letting her hair fall loose over her shoulder. "Not only have you gained power yourself, but you now have a little army of undead who follow you devotedly." Her tone is playful as her hands come to rest on the pommel of the leaning sword. When her slender fingers slowly brush the metal, Eber's eyes begin to open. She draws the blade towards her. "I wonder how long until you overthrow the King himself?" She states towards the air, off in her own world of impish humor. In the silence that falls after her words, her eyes drift down to him, seeing him looking back at her. His dark eyes glide from her down to the sword in her hands. Following his eyes, she looks to her hands over the pommel. In the silent moment, the subtle hum of metal lifts from the weapon once again. With a hint of remorse, she leans the sword back against the bed, slipping a last finger from the metal. "…Sorry." Her voice has a moment of earnest pitch before turning from the blade and rounding the bed.

The bed dips as she sets a knee to it, tugging at the covers. She nestles neath the covers, into the pillow as though the spot were hers, or had been at one time. Her eyes close as she nuzzles her face into the pillow and commits to sleep beside him, his own eyes shutting once more.

More of the night drifts by, the waves at the shore below the house gently washing against the sand. The flowers and plant life along the hill, up the path to the house, leisurely swaying from the cool breeze.

His senses more aware in current times, Eber wakes, his eyes opening slowly and drifting down his body to Lorelei's arm she is gradually gliding over him. In witless sleep, she leaves her pillow to nestle against him, resting her head to his shoulder. In time, his eyes move from her hand on his chest to her face framed by her untamed dry hair.

Studying her face, he sees subtle lines around her eyes and mouth he has watched her gain over the years. Some years that were better than others. Years when those lines were smaller. When much else was different. In his reflections, he separates his hands and moves one to hers, grasping it. Slowly, he lifts her hand to the hilt of the leaning sword, he wraps his hand over hers to hold it loosely to the handle. Mildly, his dead eyes on her change as feeling starts to accompany the thoughts of the past.

Púca – Of Celtic origin. Resembling an Alp in its impish behavior and shape shifting ability, a Púca is a fairy type being that is commonly seen as a black horse with flowing mane and luminescent eyes. However, unlike an Alp, a Púca is not known to consume blood. They are creatures that enjoy scaring people, but become loyal should they find a person with whom they bond. It was once told of a Púca that transformed itself into a large black steed that carried its human King into battle for his Kingdom.

Just as the sun has now risen, the soldiers gather in one of the military stables lined with black and grey horses, yet to be loosed to their pastures. Eber stands in the middle of the isle with his arms folded as Koza is the first to ask the Gypsy, "So why are we here? It is but only a few hours before we are to leave Lovitură. Should we not be preparing for the journey?"

The woman walks to one of the large stalls with a grey mare, then turns to Koza. "This is preparing." She beckons with an outstretched finger. "Come." He steps up to the stall and passes her a doubting glance. "Holy Water reacts to your body like it mistakes you for a Saint. You are able to fool God, but can you fool his creatures?" The Woman pulls open the door and Koza cautiously proceeds into the stall. He holds out a flat hand to the mare that gradually begins to smell him. He shuffles closer through the straw when, of a sudden, the mare's eyes flare wide and she rears to the rafters, kicking out her strong legs at the Captain. Koza hurls himself back out of the steed's domain as Lorelei shuts the door in an instant to keep the riled mare from charging out after him.

Koza sits on the cobbled floor of the isle bracing himself with his palms, panting. He looks up at the Gypsy. "And what is this to teach us?"

She looks to the Commander. "What horses will be used for this trip?"

"The four in the back." Eber nods his head the direction beyond the Gypsy. "The grey and the roan will be mounted and the two black Drafts will pull the carriage."

"And their tack?" she wanders a glance over the leather wears. Eber walks to the sectioned tack that had been set out from the rest and waves a hand at it. The Gypsy takes her bag to the tack and sets it down at the first saddle. Opening it, she pulls out vine-like weeds and begins winding it around the bridles.

"What is that?" the bald man asks.

"It is Wire Vine." She winds it tightly so it cannot be seen easily apart from the leather. "It is a weed with a strong scent to animals. With it, a horse will travel through treacherous lands guarded by large mountain cats, through battlefields that reek of death all without the single throw of a head." She holds up the first finished bridle. "With the Wire Vine they will not be able to smell you." Koza raises his head with enlightenment, realizing just how experienced the Gypsy woman is, and how he has every reason to put all his faith in her. "Which of the two cobs will be yours Commander?" she returns to weaving the vine.

"It does not matter."

Upon that, there is a nicker of disagreement that comes from a stall down the way. Lorelei pays heed to the call and walks the row of stalls coming to a majestic coal black Friesian standing sixteen hands at least. The stallion preens his head and snorts hot breath, commanding attention. "Cerny." The Gypsy breathes his name knowing the muscled beast in an instant.

The soldiers watch closely and she glides a subdued glance over her shoulder to Eber who's remaining by the tack. She pulls the latch in a single movement and releases the stallion. The black beast runs from the stall and down the isle, preening and shaking his head lofting his long mane in utter self-worth. He pounds one feathered hoof after the other onto the cobble floor, sending Koza, Thayer and Ermanno scrambling for the wall to keep from his way. Cerny slows to a trot and comes full stop in front of Eber.

The horse flares his nostrils and heaves his large lungs to show his readiness for any task asked of him by his master. Lorelei grins and strolls back to Eber, inspecting the steed as she passes by.

"Cerny is unaffected by the change of your scent." She stops when shoulder to shoulder with Eber. "It seems he will always accept you as his master."

Making no motion to touch the stallion, the Commander stands with arms folded accepting the nearness of Cerny's bowed and nudging head. "He is getting old and cannot make such journeys anymore." Cerny puffs air from his nose in rebuttal.

Quickly, Lorelei takes hold of Cerny's head, nuzzling his face. "Do not listen to this cruel man! You are strong, and brave, and have many years left of adventure." The horse nickers softly to the woman.

Eber releases a sigh. "Very well."

Excitedly, Lorelei spouts, "Wonderful! I shall return to weaving the vines for the others."

Koza and the men watch Lorelei pass by, then look back to Eber, and see Cerny raise his muzzle to nibble his lips at the side of Eber's head. Shifting his gaze to the horse, Eber's subtle annoyance fades. "…Stop it." Cerny's flopping lips in Eber's hair continue.

KAPITEL XIII

Lorelei rubs Cerny's velvet nose as he nickers his pleasure
while standing in front of the church in the Northeast
Square, tacked and ready for the journey. Eber observes no
fearful reactions to the soldiers' scent from the hitched
team or Koza's grey cob. He gives little regard to Lorelei
and Cerny's public display of affections. "Cerny, you are a
good boy, yes you are. You are a strong stallion. Always
first into battle, yes you are," she nuzzles her nose into the
soft velvet of his.

Eber turns his attention on them. "Speaking to him like
that will make him timid." He disparages the lovers.

"Really?"

"Yes."

She steps to face him eye to eye, then bends forward
slightly and puts her hands on her knees. "Eber, you are a
good boy, yes you are. You are a strong stallion. Always
first into battle, yes you are." Eber stares at her vacantly.
She straightens up and puts a finger to her lips. "Hmmm,
you do not look timid to me." Cerny nickers behind
Lorelei as Eber continues staring at her vacantly.

"Alright! Get it packed best you can." A middle-aged
priest in a black cloak tells a handful of young men who
by their attire seek to be respectable men of the cloth, but
have become merely minions instead. The young men
hoist absolute rubbish up onto the roof of the carriage.

Eber comes to the priest's side at the coach. "What is
this?" the man's dark eyes give but a momentary look at
the soldier.

One of the young men hands up a heavy gold seat plated with fine jewels to another young man on top of the carriage. "Take care with that!" the black cloaked priest barks. In their joint effort, the two young men manage the stool to the roof.

"What is this?" the Commander inquires more forcefully. The man turns without a glance Eber's way and begins to leave. Eber grabs the back of the man by his cloak and slams his face up against the coach, smashing his features rather unpleasantly. All look on at the sight of the Commander lending punishment, but only his men and Lorelei know the significance of his laying hands on a priest. If Eber burned from the touch of Lorelei's cross, then what sanctified potency will a priest have against him? "When I speak, you pay heed, or pay dearly." Of a sudden, there is a small burning pain that begins spreading in the hand Eber is using to force the priest to the side of the coach. As though putting his hand farther into the flames of a campfire, the burning pain grows the longer he holds the priest. Seeming to be ignoring the pain entirely, the Commander does not loosen his grip.

Lorelei, watching for the agony she knows Eber is dismissing, begins to part her lips and speak when a booming voice comes from the grand church steps. "That is enough, Soldat!" all turn to the man descending whose age is later forties. He wears robes of rich fabrics, colors of gold and cream. His hair is medium blond and cut short to his head with deep blue eyes that express loathing at every turn. When Ambrozij Kasimir reaches the bottom of the steps and halts at the carriage, he stands equal height with the Commander. He raises his head up and looks down his nose with the fingers of both his hands entwined as though his peace and serenity is supreme. "Kindly remove your hand from Father Andrea Biagio." Eber holds his gaze on Kasimir for a moment, then lets Biagio loose, the man straightening his attire in revolt.

The Commander pulls his paining hand somewhat behind him so as not to raise alarm should it show injury from touching the priest. "If you wish to get to Hieb in a quick pace, I would suggest you remove your refuse." He recommends.

Kasimir peruses up at the roof, then looks back to the man before him. "It is not refuse, they are all items that I need."

"For comfort or purpose?"

"Comfort is purpose, General," Kasimir informs the uncivilized barbarian commander.

"The horses will labor with the weight."

The head of the church walks by Eber and surveys the horse flesh, slapping a hand on the muscled shoulder of one of the drafts. As he turns to confront the soldier, his eye is caught by the familiar face of the woman. He pauses, surveying the woman's flesh, but refrains from a slap of his hand on her. "The horses seem strong enough to me."

Kasimir heads for the carriage door. "Now, no more discussions, let us be on our way." He makes for the coach door, which is hastily opened by Biagio.

The priest climbs into the coach and Eber passes a look to Thayer and Ermanno sitting atop the carriage ready to proceed, then gestures at Koza for him to mount his horse. As the men in the coach begin settling themselves, Eber opens the door wide. Lorelei lifts her skirt and enters the coach and takes a seat opposite the holy men, plopping her skirt and hands to her lap, and chucking a chipper look around. The men in the coach stare at her.

"What is the meaning of this?" Kasimir questions. With an uncaring stare, Eber shuts the door and mounts Cerny commanding the voyage to begin. With a lurch, the carriage starts rolling and eyes glance back and forth on the inside. "So, where are you headed exactly?" Kasimir speaks with a grumble as if fearing the answer.

She turns to him with a loving smile and loathing in her beautiful blue spheres of mischief. "Hieb." Kasimir lowers his head and flexes the stringy muscles in his jaw while staring at her from under his brow. "What is the matter your Holy Majesty? I remember a time when you sought my… company." A chuckle starts low in her throat and unsettles the thin faced man, which in turn puts Biagio on guard.

KAPITEL XIV

Ustrel – Of Bulgarian origin. An undead that preys primarily on cattle. It is known as the spirit of a recently deceased, unbaptized child. Supposedly, the creature rests in its grave for four days and nights, then rises to feed. Eating on separate victims each night, it no longer needs to return to its grave after the tenth person to die at its hands.

After leaving the city and being firmly set on their way, Biagio stretches his arms and removes the heavy black cloak in an attempt to be more comfortable. He reveals himself to be clothed in yet more black with a long sleeved fabric jerkin that if he were standing would hem at mid-thigh and a linen shirt with trousers that cover his booted shoes.

When he flexes the jerkin by reaching and stuffing the cloak in the storage below the seat, Lorelei catches sight of an accessory that is not of Holy make. He wears a slim dagger tucked within the jerkin which she slyly takes note of, then looks out the window of the coach. "Am I to assume it is by chance that you are traveling with Soldat to Hieb?" She turns to Kasimir who continues. "Or do you have a special reason you are here?"

She arches a brow at his attempt to be shrewd. "Make assumptions, your Holy Highness."

As the carriage rocks mildly back and forth along the tree lined path, their bodies sway, yet Kasimir's and Lorelei's interlocked gaze does not.

Four days later, the journey had so far taken the travelers deep into the forests of Der Vorfahr. Over bridges, through shallow streams, over hills and through dangerously narrow paths, they stayed focused in their long exhaustive adventure.

Biagio flops open a small map of Der Vorfahr and begins to study it. "Do you know where we are?" Kasimir sighs.

Using his finger as a pointer, Biagio replies, keeping his eyes entranced with the wandering lines that indicate mountains. "Let's see, we have traveled through the Alter Forest without consequence... and chose the Yore path to the right rather than Sowie to the left..."

"How much farther is it we have to go?" Kasimir takes a deep breath, dreading the answer.

"A ways."

As the clattering coach rounds a bend, they come upon a lone vardo wagon stuck in mud off the path with five gypsy men rocking and pushing in try to get it out. As Kasimir's carriage passes, Lorelei watches the scene with little note, then an idea flashes through her mind. "Stop the coach!" she yells out the window.

Recognizing her voice instantly, Eber halts Cerny and in turn what follows behind him. With a deep sigh, he stares down at the neck of his horse, contemplating the thorn that's going to be jabbed into his side. The Gypsy steps down out of the coach as Eber approaches. "What is it?" His tone is not happy while he remains mounted.

Lorelei looks up to him. "They are my people, Eber." She turns toward the group in need. "We shall help them."

Eber rests his hand on Cerny's withers with a stare. She glances to him and disperses her smirk, replacing it with raised eyebrows and a look that demands compliance. "Koza, Ermanno... go help her people." Cerny stomps a hoof on the ground at delay he now has to endure.

Koza dismounts from his horse and Ermanno, who's up by Thayer at the reins, hops off the coach in pursuit of the woman as she walks to the other gypsies. "My fellow Romani!" she outstretches her arms.

One of the men, Koza's height, but 10 plus his age steps up to Lorelei. "Greetings."

"Would you care for some assistance?"

"Unfortunately, it is a lost cause." He throws a hand toward the vardo. "I don't think the extra men will even help." He looks to Koza and Ermanno over her shoulder.

She smiles. "Let us see." She turns to the soldiers and points a hand to the wagon. "If you would?"

Koza steps up to one side of the back while Ermanno rounds to the other. "Don't forget to lift with your spine," Ermanno laughs. Koza sets Ermanno's stupid humor aside and counts down from three, then with Ermanno helping they push the wagon free from the mud.

The gypsies stand baffled at the feat. "It appears two more helped," She grins.

"Is there a way to repay you? In the vardo, I have some fine fabrics perhaps you would like."

With a tone that is more true to her, she says, "I have no care for fabrics, but to bring grief to one I dislike? That would be a good exchange." She narrows her eyes with a smile.

"Who do you dislike?"

"Ambrozij Kasimir. He is in that coach and those are his things upon it."

The man looks to the roof of the carriage, "He has riches like I have never seen."

Hushed, she continues to speak. "And to think all that guards those riches are four soldiers."

He turns back to her with a smile that says he is no fool. "But I have seen what two of them can do."

"They are the strongest. The one in the driver's seat is young, inexperienced, fragile, even afraid." She glances behind her to see Eber's watchful and annoyed eyes on her from atop Cerny. "And that one… incompetent."

The man surveys Eber closely. "I like his sword." Lorelei's eyes have a moment of betrayal to her play, the idea of that sword being a prize something she finds little humor in. "When he is dead, it will be mine."

"Dead?" she says with a touch of amusement.

"You say he is incompetent, then he will be easy to kill," the man grins.

"Yeees." Her tone grows a little more amused.

"Woman," Eber calls. "It is time we move." Cerny puffs a breath from his nose with dictation. With a last nod to the men, she departs to the coach and they continue on their journey.

KAPITEL XV

After the passing of a few hours, Kasimir hangs his head out the window. "Stop the coach!" he barks above the clop of the draft's oversized hooves on the dirt road and clang of their tack.

The General halts the coach and moves Cerny to the window. "What?"

"I cannot take one more hour inside this wagon! And I will not be satisfied by a mere respite. We are camping here for the night."

With a cocked head, the Commander comments laxly, "It does not matter to me when we arrive in Hieb."

The carriage pulls off the narrow road and comes to a rest at the treeline. Straying off to the side, Eber dismounts Cerny and stands with his arm leisurely across the saddle. Koza hops down off his horse and tracks to the coach door, opening it wide for the passengers' departure. As Kasimir begins to rise and come for the exit, Koza gives him a reminder of manly duty. "If you remember Sir, there is a lady present," the Gypsy turns her head and looks over the young soldier judgingly. "She should be first to exit."

Koza holds up her hand to be taken for assistance and Lorelei begins stepping from the coach taking it. Because of the folding drapery of her skirt, she does not see Kasimir hook her foot with his own. She falls from the door and is caught by Koza's embrace. For a moment, she looks up at the young man as he looks down at her, then he becomes self-aware of Eber's surveying gaze and sets her back more on her feet, drawing his hands from any touch on her.

As Kasimir departs to the last step of the coach, Lorelei looks back at him from the corner of her eye and slides her hand to Koza's hilt. She pushes the handle of the short sword back, forcing the other end to stick out tripping the Head of the Church. He becomes a heap of cream colored cloth face first on the ground. "How kind of you, your Holy Majesty, to bless our campgrounds with a kiss!" She holds her hands together in front of her and plays the role of Holy admirer with a smile, then she grabs two hands full of her skirt and steps over the man. Biagio comes quickly from the carriage and assists his leader to his feet. The woman walks, aimed for the Commander's side. As Kasimir takes Biagio's hand, his spiteful glare hooks onto the Gypsy and he begins to make for the woman. Lorelei stops and turns to face the aura of hatred she senses is coming up behind her.

"You ought to be punished for your insolence!" Kasimir stares into her eyes. "To mock me is to mock God! You should be tied to one of the wheels of that carriage and whipped!"

Lorelei smirks. "You are right, Kasimir." She turns to Eber. "And the fierce and merciless Commander Soldat will surely be the one to bind me to the wheel?" she grins at Eber who then turns his back and begins uncinching Cerny, trying his best to avoid the ordeal. Lorelei looks to the other soldiers and calls out. "Then, one of you brave warriors will attempt to punish me?!"

Koza says on the move, "I'm going to unhitch the horses." Ermanno and Thayer follow with murmurs of anxious offerings of assistance.

With calm amusement, Lorelei steps up close to Kasimir who does not seem as bothered by the nearness of a woman's body than the Head of the Church should be. "It seems, your Holy Highness, that if you wish me punished you must do it yourself." Lorelei's words have a knack at tantalizing a man's thoughts to focus on every subtle motion of her lips.

Kasimir draws himself back from her distractions and throws his frustration in another direction. "Remove my things from the coach!" he demands of the Commander's men. Thayer and Ermanno come to stand in proximity of Koza as they all simply stare at the Holy Majesty. "What are you gawking for?! I have told you what to do!"

Ermanno moves up to Kasimir while rubbing his chin. "There is just one problem."

"What?!"

With a grin firmly set, he continues, "You are not our Commander."

Kasimir looks back at Eber who in wake of a brief pausing second retorts, "Koza."

"Yes Sir?"

"Retrieve his refuse from the carriage." Kasimir grimaces. Koza, being the only one of the soldiers able to touch items of sanctity, makes for the corner of the coach to climb up. The General begins walking farther into what will be the campsite with the Gypsy whilst Ermanno and Thayer continue unhitching the horses where Koza left off.

After a fire has been lit to a pile of fallen branches and sticks, Kasimir sits on his bejeweled golden stool, picking through the choice of foods he has brought on the trip. "This is going to be a long journey." Eber remarks as he stands a distance from the fire, behind the Gypsy who is sitting on a downed tree. They are both looking at Kasimir and his fastidiousness.

Koza comes to stand by his leader and the woman. "Would you care to have a fresh fish to eat?" he asks Lorelei.

Lorelei nods her head with a smile as she stands holding her heavy red wrap around her. "That would be delicious."

Koza gestures the proper direction and she starts walking ahead of him. "I'll guard her closely, Sir," the Captain dutifully says to Eber, who doesn't pass him a single glance of caring. Receiving no reaction from his Commander, Koza shifts his gaze and walks after her.

Koza helps Lorelei down a rocky ledge. "So how is it that you know where the fish are?" She inquires.

He sets her to her feet. "I can smell them, even in the water." They arrive at a clear swift moving river.

"It must be the Upir in you," she chaffs.

As they sit apart from one another, she watches the Captain as he removes his boots and stands taking off his black short waist uniform coat and white shirt to fish by hand from the river. After wading into the shallow, he waits patiently. Time passes and finally a topic of discussion comes to the surface. Restraining the bulk of his fascination Koza asks simply, "So how long have you known the Commander?" With her seemingly persistent humor about everything, she chuckles softly. "What do you laugh at?"

"Ask what you truly want to know."

The current flows around his knees and the water ripples his reflection as he contemplates the tact he will give to that question she speaks of. "What are you?"

She sits on a large rock with her chin resting in the palm of her hand as her elbow sets down on crossed legs. "What do you think I am?"

Koza feels he can continue as her behavior is not that of aggression, but playfulness. "Something powerful."

"Ooo, why do you say that?"

"Because of the way the Commander is with you." She arks a brow. "To you he shows respect... I am not used to seeing that." She chuckles softly. "I cannot tell if he fears you, or... if it is another reason you are special to him?"

"Are we lovers you mean to ask?" He looks at her, a little resistant to show his true curiosity. "...No." She reflects, her eyes cast low. "Love is not a part of it... Not anymore."

Hearing the sound of memories in her voice, Koza watches her drift to another world. "Then he fears you?"

She looks up and smiles. "Do you think that man fears anything?"

"...No." Steadily, Koza returns to his fishing, receiving no true answers to his questions.

KAPITEL XVI

Vourdalak – Of Muscovian origin. Not much is known about this being except for the fact that she is an evil yet beautiful woman. Her deceptive ways are death for handsome young men whom she deems worthy of being her prey.

Pushing open the heavy wooden door to the old tavern, young Lorelei's small hand slips off the handle as she comes in from outside. The door clicks loudly in its latch as she pulls her shawl more up around her, shaking her shoulders free of the bit of snow.

The sounds of people talking draw her eyes around the room. Farmers, blacksmiths, shop owners all talking with the women the little tavern has to offer. What captures her eye most, are the few soldiers making themselves at home. Black cloth uniforms with sections of smooth leather, the styles more telling of rank than fashion among the Der Vorfahr army. It is strange to see King Berin's soldiers in a village like this. Der Vorfahr soldiers wear their uniforms when in Loviturä, in war, or on special missions. Having heard no warring and knowing this rotten village is far from the fabled glory of Loviturä, it all leads Lorelei to think the men have a more specialized reason for being here.

She moves past the men and women for the bar of the tavern. The tender of the tavern and owner of it is wiping at the counter when he halts, seeing her approach. She instantly turns up a smile to hide anything her face might have been saying beforehand. "Hello, Arron."

"Lorelei." He says her name in pain.

"It is going to be a cold night. I shall have a bottle of your finest." The girl pats her hands on the counter, smiling innocently.

"The finest, is expensive."

"I do not have any money."

He replies coldly, "I know that." Her smile fades and the tender clears his throat. "But… I cannot afford another rat infestation." Grabbing a bottle, he sets it to the bar in front of her. "Take this, and your curses elsewhere, Gypsy." Her smile returns and she snatches the bottle. Turning on her heels, she is met with a couple soldiers in her path.

"Hello." One leans forward.

The other does the same. "You look much younger than the other women here." He glances over them. "And you are pretty."

Shifting her expression from poor tolerance, Lorelei grows a smile and tilts her head into her wavy hair, playing at her youth. "Would you like to have a drink with us?"

"I...I suppose." She touches a finger to her lip like a child thinking on what they are and are not allowed to do. The young men motion for her to aim for their table.

Taking a seat between them, Lorelei scoots closer to the table. Setting the bottle on the surface, one of the men takes hold of it. "Let's have our drink."

Her eyes widen and she grabs it from him, in a quick moment, showing her true contempt for the soldiers with a glare. At once, she shifts again to her play of innocent youth. "I have to take this back to my mommy. She is sick and she says booze makes it all better." The men glance at each other, having an idea of how sick the woman is.

"Your mother is sick?" One of the men chuckles. "Is it catching?"

Lorelei sits with the bottle between her legs, staring at it. "No… That is what the doctor with the strange wax mask said anyway." The men jump from their seats by her, her lips curling to a more honest smile.

Of a sudden, the tavern door opens, a soldier slamming it to the wall as he enters. Soon, the man steps to the side and another soldier comes in the door frame. The falling snow blows in with him, the specks of white covering his black uniform of cloth and leather. Leather, Lorelei notes is a different pattern than the others. The man with black wavy hair and scraggle on his jawline begins to look around the room that has grown dead silent. The simple motion from this young man brings the soldiers in the tavern to their feet, their faces losing all levity on them moments ago from drinks and women in their hands.

Casting lingering examinations on those drinks... and women, the man speaks. "Good to see you all have priorities." One of the men at Lorelei's side swallows harshly, his body rigid at attention. Glancing up, she lifts a heavy brow at his behavior. He acts fearful, yet when she looks back at the man as he begins to walk towards the bar, all she sees is a soldier like them. Granted, his presence is the most commanding of any of them in the room, and granted, the leather on his uniform suggests a different rank, like perhaps a higher officer, and granted, he is much better looking, her thoughts pause. In a second pass of her eyes up and down the officer, her eyes set on something which instantly sets the soldier apart from any other for certain. As the young man moves by the table for the bar, past the sway of his arm, she sees held to his hip, a sword. The weapon is known to her without doubt. The long handle ended by a round silver pommel, the crossguard, two curving pieces of silver tipped by their own round balls.

Stopping at the bar, the soldier focuses on the tender. "Ladislas Dimas." The barkeep grimaces at the name even Lorelei recognizes. "Where is he?" The soldier asks, his tone telling the tender for what purpose he wishes to know.

"...I...I do not know."

Seeing the man simply stare at him in a moment of silence, Arron slowly curves his brows, instinctively moving his head into his shoulders. "Take a breath, Keep."

The soldier advises. "Look at me well… Should you lie to me?" The tender gulps that breath.

"Please," he chokes out softly.

"Dimas… Where?" The soldier simplifies.

"I…I…"

"Ladislas Dimas?" Lorelei leans past the soldier, her hair hanging as she stares up at him. The men at the bar lower their locked eyes to her. "I know where he is," she smiles.

"Lorelei!" the tender barks. With that, the soldier glances up, then back at her, the man's reaction saying she is not lying.

The young gypsy grins, straightening her body at the soldier's side. "He is leading an uprising against King Berin, that is why you and your soldiers are here, yes? To kill him?" Her smile holds.

"Lorelei Zima, if you say another word, I will-"

Whipping her head to the threat, she shows its welcome. "Careful Arron, perhaps next time, it will be more than rats." Taking her expression as seriously as the soldier's before, Arron closes his lips together, anger speaking in his eyes instead. She twists back to the soldier, hands held sweetly behind her. "Now, back to Dimas. I will take you to him if you like."

The soldier's dark eyes soften, having favor for an easier way than burning down the tavern to get his answers. "Would you?"

"Of course!... For a fee." She leans. Once more checking the tavern owner for the way he is glaring at the young woman, the soldier is more certain of her honesty. "Very well."

She perks, growing genuinely happy with her victory. "Perfect! You may call me Lorelei Zima." She sets a slim hand to her chest, then gesturing towards him. "What shall I call you, soldier?"

"Eber Soldat." His answer is dry and factual.

Slowly, staring up at him, she begins to chuckle, a snort slipping out. "A soldier, named Soldier?!" Gradually, the soldiers in the tavern look to one another. Eber opens his mouth and is immediately silenced by another loud snort. Closing his mouth, he begins to wait for her eventual end.

"What fee do you charge?" He asks, her laughter finally quieting as she wipes a tear.

"What fee?" She flutters her dark heavy lashes lining her bright blue eyes casting wonder up to him. Again, she starts to play an ignorant child, touching her lip in thought. "Hmm." She begins to circle him, looking his body up and down. "What do you have that I would want?" Coming back round his front, she looks to the sword at his side. After holding her gaze on it, she blinks away. "I will take your sword." She waves a hand, the fee made like a passing thought.

"...No." His reply is cleanly cut.

"No?!" She flinches. "But it is just a sword." She brushes at the air in front of the blade on his hip. She grabs at the hilt, wobbling it.

Leisurely, Eber's hand lifts, gripping lightly over hers on the handle and removing it. "Do not touch me... Please." Pouting her lips, her brows curve with irritation, being told what to do. Defiantly, she pokes his chest with a finger, holding it to him and her eyes a dead stare into his. After a pause, he lets out a deep breath and looks around the tavern. "Would anyone else accept a fee?"

"Fine," she grumbles, folding her arms. "I will take what you give me. It better be money." She glares at him sideways. Reaching in his coat, he brings out four coins from an inner pocket. Her eyes widen at the sight of shiny metal. "Gold?"

"The purest. You may have all four of them." Her eyes sparkle up to him. Eagerly, she holds up her hands to which he sets one piece.

"You said all of them." She frowns.

"One fourth, for one fourth of the way. When we are there, you will have them all." Turning from her sneer, he tells, "Come."

Into the snow, the soldiers come from the tavern, their horses waiting at posts outside. Atop a brown steed with a couple mounted soldiers at his sides, an older man sits, his hands resting on his horse's withers.

"Well?" General Krow asks, his aged voice gruff in texture.

"The bar owner, nor others wish to be of assistance, Sir." Coming down the steps into the street, Eber passes one of the horses, its black mane laying over it's black neck, its fur thick from the approaching winter, its sharp hoof pawing at the ice, strong muscle flexing under its velvet coat. "However, this girl knows where Dimas is and she will lead us there." Casually, Lorelei comes to the steps, her attention drawn by the pawing animal, puffing hot breath from its nostrils.

"Very good, see that any men who are drunk from their choice of duties they wished to carry out over my orders, are left behind. And cut the girths of their saddles. If they like it here so much, they may stay." The old man lifts the reins of his horse, moving the animal along.

"Yes, Commander." Looking to one of the soldiers, Eber barks, "Jorin!" The named man snaps to his attention, sitting on his horse. "The girl will ride with you."

Lorelei turns her head to examine the average looking man. "No," she informs, looking back to the horse nuzzling on his muzzle. "I will ride with you, Soldier."

"No, my horse only cares for me. He would trample you if given a chance."

"Which one is your horse?"

Eber turns, seeing Lorelei rubbing on the stallion's nose, kissing at the air in front of his muzzle, his puffs of breath calmed and pawing ceased as Cerny merely enjoys her affection. "That one." He gawks.

Blinking, Lorelei looks back to Cerny, cupping his large round jowls and cooing to him. "Are you vicious? You are vicious aren't you?" Cerny nickers, nudging his head forward to her. Eber's haze of confusion at what he is seeing yet does not believe passes slowly as his brows lift and he lets out a breath.

KAPITEL XVII

The paths change as village roads turned to wooded trails become mountain passes. Pointing the way with each bit of terrain they cross, Lorelei leads the soldiers through the woods for the distant mountains farther away.

The snow falls and winds blow, howling through the passes and down valleys. The trek summoning more and more strength from the horses as the drifts of white are getting deeper and deeper.

With the fall of the snow, the fall of the sun has made the mountain side colder. The last of the booze in some of the mens' blood is the only heat they feel.

The horses push through the snow, one or two stumbling and catching themselves. Commander Krow's steed struggles as he leads the group of soldiers through the storm. One sturdy hoof after the other, Cerny climbs the covered trails. His head up, his mane whips, his eyes on what is ahead without yield.

The night moves as little of it is seen in the sky through the blizzard. The men frost bitten, are growing more tired. Farther ahead from the group, Cerny sways as he moves more assuredly through the drifts lulling Lorelei. Her heavy lids lower, her head starting to hang. Gradually, her body sets against Eber's back, her face nestling in the soft fabric of his coat. Glancing back, Eber notes her tiredness as she nuzzles into his back, the men coming up the hill not looking much more awake or alert. Suddenly, what awareness her sleepy mind still has, Lorelei jerks back up right, catching Eber's eye, showing a twinge of embarrassment that the soldier's shoulder blade was needed for a moment.

A soft tug on Cerny's reins brings the animal to a stop, his eagerness to continue showing in a somewhat antsy stance. "General Krow!" Eber calls over the winds. The man halts, turning his horse enough to look back. "We should rest, wait for the storm to pass so we do not lose ourselves in the blizzard."

Looking around him, the depth of the snow drifts numbing his horse's legs, the bite of the cold air on his older bones, he nods in agreement. "Take care of sentries."

Eber complies. "Kalls!" The soldier rides up. "Take point watch." The soldier nods to the orders given him with a frown, urging his horse on ahead up the path. "Now let us find a place to rest."

A couple of the men having found a carved out hill nestled into the mountain, Eber watches the soldiers make their way into the cave-like cover. While some tie lines between trees for the horses, others unsaddle said horses, hauling the tack and blankets into the dry camp inside where others have started fires, hidden well inside the rock. Krow moves for the mouth of the cave, rubbing at a hip whilst another soldier bothers with the man's tack.

Crouching, Lorelei digs happily at the snow, bearing a few blades of green that Cerny is grateful to see, nickering to her as he munches at them. She stands and watches him eat, patting his thick neck.

"Jorin." The man stops at the call from Eber. "You will take the first watch outside."

"Yes Sir." He wearily makes his way up the hillside to fashion his own little camp for warmth.

Training his attention on Cerny, Eber tugs at the saddle straps, loosening the tack and pulling it from the horse. Watching him, Lorelei pulls the bridal over Cerny's ears while he chews, holding his head low for her to reach his crop. Eber takes the bridal from her and the single rope to the halter around Cerny's head still in her hands, nodding towards the cave. "Go inside." Cerny watches her go, nickering to her the farther she disappears into the mountain. "Do not embarrass yourself," Eber comments to his horse, yanking the blanket from his back. Swinging his head, Cerny nips at Eber's side, a clump of coat and shirt in his mouth. "Ow!" Eber jerks, Cerny returning to the nibbles of frozen grass, blamelessly.

Lorelei steps into the cave, looking over her options of where to take a seat. The soldiers make small gatherings around a fire, talking among themselves, some of them making their beds out of the saddles and blankets from their horses. Her vision pans to that of Krow dominating his spot by one of the fires.

Not very pleased with her choices, Lorelei stands unmoving until Eber passes behind her. Catching him from the corner of her eye, she scurries along after him.

He drops the saddle and blanket to the rocks, paying little mind to her presence. "I would say the storm is not passing any time soon."

"Your Tarot cards tell you that?"

"I do not have cards," she grumbles, not liking his snarky tone. "I use sticks." She holds up said items from the pouch hanging on her hip, beneath the blanket shawl around her.

He stares momentarily at the sticks in her small hand. "That is not more legitimate."

Letting out a puff, she brushes off her frustrations. "Tell me soldier named Soldier, would you like me to read your fortune?"

He pulls his sheath from his sword belt, not moving his eyes from hers. "At this rate, I cannot afford it." Her eyes lower from his to watch the sword as he places it against a boulder. Eber takes a seat by the saddle, starting to wrap the bridal with its reins.

Plopping to a seat by him, Lorelei sets her hands to her ankles as she folds her legs, staring at the sword leaning against the large rock. "I do not see the value in that old thing." Wanting some answers in her mind for questions she has, she asks, "how did you come to get that sword anyway?"

"It was a battlefield, the end of a war," he tells casually, his attention on the bridal. "A soldier had managed to survive the thick of the battle, death all around him and there he stood with that sword in hand. We came to learn he was the enemy army's commander. He had proven himself formidable and I was tasked with killing him. I am certain Krow expected me to die trying."

Lorelei smirks, looking him over. "You surprised him."

"It seems for all his skill, I was better." Assumption of the soldier's abilities and threat, something Lorelei had made plenty of back in the tavern, first seeing that sword at his side. "When I looked at his blade, it had no abrasions, no nicks. The blade was perfect as though newly made and it had been through war."

Beginning to accept the seeming reality that his sword will stay his, "There is legend of a long blade forged by angels in heaven and wielded by Lucifer against those angels when he rose against God, cast from heaven to fall with him. The fable says the sword did not fall all the way to Hell with him; that the weapon came to earth, found by man. Once used to war with angels, Romhild now battles in the wars of the lesser man, her just fate to be held by one who is more than man." Growing solemn, Eber listens to her tales of some history perhaps partly true. "My father was a fool to hand that sword of yours over in that bargain. The day that enemy captain you killed came to him, bartering gold for a means to be powerful." Eber watches her as the more believable parts of that history become known, her father's ownership of his sword at one time, being the reason for her desire to have it back in the beginning. "Never let anyone take Romhild from you, Soldier." Lorelei shifts her focus, letting it drift away from the soldier and his weapon he earned, Eber watching her manner of knowing more than ever saying. Seeing the men pass stories to each other, she sees something else being passed to Krow. Food. A chunk of bread here and there, most likely gathered from the tavern. She licks her lips. Vaguely, Eber sees the glint in her eyes, watching the food. Dismissing her wants and needs, she says grumpily, "goodnight, Soldier." She lays down, turning over and tugging her shawl to her face while closing her eyes. Shortly, she hears rustling, knowing Eber is moving and sounding as though rising to his feet. A moment of peace passes, her eyes staying closed and lids becoming loose as the pain in her stomach is ignored while the smell of the bread seems to get closer. The sound of boots on the cave floor stirring her, she opens her eyes to a chunk of bread in front of her. Gradually, she looks over her shoulder, watching Eber reclaim his seat, then lay his head back on Cerny's saddle, interlocking his fingers over his stomach. Drifting her eyes back to the bread when laying her head down on her arm once more, she gently sets her hand on the chunk and draws it closer, plucking a small piece off and putting it between her lips. Studying each bite, that pain of emptiness begins to fade.

KAPITEL XVIII

Feeling the pass of time, Eber's eyes open and he sits up.
Checking over the cave, he finds some men asleep,
wrapped in their horses' blankets, while a few are still
awake, quietly talking by their fires. Krow rests
comfortably by one of the fires, his mind in slumber.
Passing the same surveillance over Lorelei, he sees she is
fast asleep, tucked into her shawl, holding what is left of
the chunk of bread.

He stands and collects his sword, latching it back to his
side before aiming out of the lair. The scrape of leather
soles on the cave floor waking her slightly, Lorelei sits up,
seeing him leaving.

Outside the cave, somewhat up the ridge, sits Jorin by a
fire. The winter winds, blocked by a flapping sheet of
cloth, strung from the ground to the trees.

"Jorin." The man snaps his back straight as he hears his
name, his body seconds from slipping off into a hunched
over nap.

"Captain!" He jumps to his feet with Eber coming up the
ridge. Down the way between the horse lines, Cerny stirs,
looking up to watch Eber pass by.

"I am relieving you." Pleased, Jorin gives a 'yes Sir' and
darts along for the warmer place. Cerny's head follows the
man down the ridge. The horse lets out a puff of hot breath
as his eyes and head then follows Lorelei up the ridge.
Eber takes his seat by the fire, drawing his sword from its
belt and resting it against his shoulder. Movement catching
his attention, he looks to see Lorelei flop a blanket on the
cold ground by the fire and him. She sets down her chunk

of bread and locks eyes with him, lowering to her knees on the blanket, then plopping to her side.

Seeing she favors his company over others, even in the cold of outside, he looks forward at the fire, keeping quiet and uninterested in her presence, what he assumes has earned that favor. She opens her eyes, looking into the forest. "Tell me Soldier, do you think all women are whores?" Her manner turned away from him, like her body.

He stares at the fire. "What does it matter what I think, Girl?"

"...I am just curious."

Eber reflects on his life, its current state and its beginning. "I am the son of a whore, a woman whose child was the result of her earnings, not love, or desire to be a mother."

A thought passing through her mind, Lorelei rolls to her back, her bright blue eyes continuing up to him. "In that case, I would think you are far more predisposed to think women whores."

Coldly, he expresses the ideals his birth has given him. "I do not like weak people. Whores are weak women who have let men put them in that position."

She hears his seriousness, his opinions from an impacted childhood of damaged upbringing, and respects it with, "They let men put them in many positions, the good ones anyways." She punctuates with a chuckle at her humor that turns to a snort.

Blinking, Eber lifts a brow, looking her way. "...You are... odd."

Her head rolls to him, her hair bunching on the ground under her cheek. "And you are a man who does not like whores... You are... a freak." She gives a couple small laughs, turning back over to get some sleep. Having a moment of thought over her words and her play with him,

Eber looks back to the flames, a lift of his lips into the corner of his mouth leading to one soft chuckle.

The middle of the night blusters, the winds swirling small funnels of snow at times.

Letting out a small grunt of frustration, Lorelei sits up, her hair messily around her face and shawl dropping down. Passing a glance on Eber, he looks from the woods to her. Lifting to her feet, her glance turns more to a glare at him. "I will be back." Wrapping her shawl around her tightly, she starts to leave the small camp.

"Do not venture far," he somewhat orders.

Stopping, she turns. "I will go where I wish to pee." Turning back, she heads into the dark from the fire, Eber's expression not changing from his stare over the flames.

In the darkness of the woods, the winds howl as the only sounds through the dark trees of nearly black bark with snow matted to the side of each one. Straightening her skirt, Lorelei brushes at the snow it drug through. She aims back for the small camp, heading for the warmth she left.

A few steps and she stops, her eyes fixed on the path through the trees back to the faint light of the fire over the hill. Her pause is not from what she sees, what she hears being only the winds, but what she feels is different. Her bright blue eyes begin to pan the trees. That feeling building in her the longer she hunts the woods, of a sudden, a wide hand wraps round to her mouth, muffling a surprised scream as she jumps and is jerked away.

The sense of time moves by and the longer Eber stares at the fire, the more he realizes the longer he stares at the fire. Steadily, a feeling of his own grows inside. He stands, slipping his sword back in the loop of its belt.

Trailing the footprints quickly being covered by the snow, Eber tracks Lorelei's path. Gradually, he comes to something which gives him pause. Tracks around hers, larger than her prints, and human.

Tracking the new prints, Eber comes to a clearing of the trees, his black uniform hiding him in the treeline of black woods. It is there, he sees some men from the village yanking Lorelei along with a strip of cloth tightly around her mouth as she kicks and growls through the fabric.

"This one," Arron tells, judging one of the trees. Another man heeds the bar owner, pulling a sword at his side from its sheath enough to slice a strip of rope, something Lorelei watches. The man heaves the rope over one of the sturdier branches. Arron comes to her, drawing her attention from the other man. "You think I want to kill a young girl?" Lorelei's eyes turn up to him, showing her lack of hesitation she would have over killing a middle aged man. "But you are no girl, you are a monster. You are a consort of the Devil like your father was... Dimas does not deserve to be hunted. He is trying to help us, and when we are done with you, we will warn him what is coming."

One of the other men loops the rope over Lorelei's head, forcing a jump from her as she starts to fight again. The bar owner and other man help the third move her closer to the tree, the rope starting to be pulled taut. Setting his hand on his sword's hilt, Eber begins to take a step to intervene.

At once, Lorelei slips from the couple men, rushing towards the tree and the man holding the rope, making slack as she goes. Lunging, she lands on the man and pushes him to the ground. They tussle as the other men hurry to them, grabbing the rope. With all their strength, Arron and the other man pull at the rope, jerking it free of slack in an instant as they hoist the weight into the trees. The difference being, Lorelei has wrapped the third man's neck with the slack of rope she made running to him, the others heaving him into the tree instead of her as she slips out of the noose. Pausing, Eber's hand lowers from his sword, watching her defend herself.

The man's sword is brought to her eye level, she pulls it from its sheath, turning it. She runs it into the gut of the man helping Arron hoist their friend into the tree. The stab to his stomach, releasing his grip on the rope instantly, he drops from the wound, as she rips it from him and slices upwards at Arron. The man stands a moment before his head falls from its body, the rope sliding through his hands. Watching his head fall, the sound of it hitting the snow matches the landing of the third man pulled into the tree. Choking, the man tugs at the rope around his throat. Vaguely seeing what is in front of him, he scurries to his feet when Lorelei turns his way with his sword.

Taking to his feet, he pants as he runs for the treeline. In a blink, Lorelei's hateful burn of her blue orbs on the man turns to levity as she straightens, rips the cloth from around her mouth, and calls. "Watch your head!" At once, she scoops her toes under Arron's head, kicking it towards the treeline, its path landing with a thud on the third man, dropping him to the ground. "Oh, how silly of me," she touches her chest and smiles. "I meant watch his head."

Eber's brows lift, never having seen such methods he admittedly found... different. Casually, he turns, aiming back for the camp.

Dropping the sword, Lorelei brushing at her skirt, her manner returning to something more dark and cold, than fun and playful as she looks over the dead bodies.

Trekking into the small camp, Lorelei finds Eber watching the fire as he was when she left. He looks up to her and she stares back for a moment when her face lightens and her manner again turns to play. "Well," she drops to her knees on her blanket by the flames. "That was a relief." She flops to her side, snuggling into her shawl. "Goodnight again, Soldier." Quietly, in the small seclusion of her back being to the soldier, her playful smile straightens as she begins to stare at the blowing snow somewhat saddened by the trials not every person faces. Gradually, she reaches for her chunk of bread, bringing it closer to her.

Watching her nestle into her shawl, thoughts pass through his mind leisurely, as his dark eyes drift over her. Lorelei will never be a woman who is made weak by any man. It is a thought that shows in his eyes favorably.

In the morning, Krow's horse makes his way through the snow up the mountain passes as the soldiers follow Lorelei's directions. Telling them of their nearness to their destination, the group feels some relief, knowing the next leg of their long journey will hopefully be home.

Also thinking on that venture home the soldiers will make, Lorelei reflects on her recent life. Of people she has known, none have made such good company as the soldier named Soldier. Once he is gone, so will be the company. A part of her feels a twinge of disappointment as she looks to Eber's back.

Climbing the narrow path between the dark trees atop the ridge, Krow holds up a hand, halting his horse and those behind him. Eber draws Cerny to a stop, the animal pawing at the snow with warm breath puffing out of his nostrils. "It is the camp." Krow tells, with he and his captain looking down the ridge out into the small clearing filled with tents and supplies. "Dismount." The soldiers obey.

Swinging his leg over, Eber drops from the saddle to the layer of white powder. As Lorelei slips her leg over, she readies herself to hop off Cerny's rump, when a gesture halts her in mid-motion. Her eyes widen as Eber's hands raise to help her down. The notion is strange, it is a small action of respect, something she is not accustomed to. Carefully, she studies his eyes, hunting for mockery, or jest, but only finds him patiently waiting. With a blink, she lowers towards him, setting her hands to his arms when he grips her waist and brings her to the bed of snow. Flattening her feet, her study of him fades to a brush of her dress as he walks away.

He moves to the ridge by Krow, and she steps up between them. "Do you see Dimas?"

Looking out over the camp, she examines each man there, moving from tent to tent and task to task. "There, that is him." She points to a man coming from a large tent in a quiet place of the camp. He walks towards the river and small group of men at it's edge. Watching him focus on Dimas, Lorelei clears her throat, and growing a smirk, holds out her hand palm up. "I have brought you all the way to him, now for all the payment."

Tugging at his uniform coat, Eber reaches in for the three gold coins, setting them in her palm. Pleased, she looks them over, turning them and trailing her finger along their rim. He looks on to Krow. "How do you wish to proceed, Sir?"

The older man grouses, "Have Jorin take range with his bow on the ridge and use his marksmanship. We'll kill Dimas with a single shot."

Eber begins to study his surroundings, watching the winds blow through the trees along the ridge line. Watching the limbs sway, he replies, "The winds keep shifting, an assassination shot might be ruined, alerting his makeshift army." Krow grumbles. "A second plan?"

After a moment of thought, Krow gradually looks to Lorelei admiring her coins. "Always use your resources, Captain." Slowly, Lorelei lifts her eyes to the men.

Dimas' men in the camp halt what they are doing, seeing the young woman pass by. The men watch Lorelei walk deeper into the camp as though belonging.

Coming to the man by the river, she calls to the leader. "Dimas." His conversation with one of his rebel soldiers ceases. Slowly, he turns to look on Lorelei.

"You?" His eyes pan her frame, studying her. "What is it you want, Wretch?" His view of her is the same as a bug on a slice of pie.

Her eyes shift from irritation to play as she holds up a rolled parchment. "A message I have from Arron in the village."

"He sent you?" He reaches for the paper.

"It is urgent." She draws it quickly from his grasp.

He scowls. "Urgent?"

She waves it without care, as though the contents had no importance. "Oh, something about the Berin soldiers in the mountain, hunting you."

His eyes widen. "Give me that."

She hops back from him, the men around them growing the same look of hate for her as is building more and more on his face. "I will bargain with you for it." She smirks.

"Bargain? Why would Arron send you?"

"Because he knew I would make it through the storm… Or he hoped I would die from it?" She taps her lip. "No, that cannot be it." Her playful grin returns.

Taking a breath, he tells, "Very well, I will give you a few coins for the message." Taking off with a heavy step, he treks through the camp, Lorelei turning with him as the men around watch. At the top of the ridge, Krow's sturdy smirk follows them.

Dimas draws back the flap of his large tent, entering ahead of Lorelei and letting the flap drop back. She flinches as the canvas nearly slaps her in the face. Lowering her brows, her eyes burn through the fabric as she flings the flap to the side for herself.

She enters the tent and passes her eyes over the terrain, noting her surroundings. Frustrated, Dimas goes to a sack and rummages. "You know, you should be grateful, feel indebted to me." Lorelei lifts her eyes from the nearby table with a silver letter opener resting atop it, to the man, her expression unimpressed. "I am fighting to free people like me and you from Berin's tyranny."

She shrugs. "I do not have a problem with Berin. His laws do not affect me."

He huffs. "If you lived by laws, they would. A wretch does not belong to any nation or its laws." Coldly watching the man's back, Lorelei's lips curl. "Here." He tosses a few coins to the floor at her feet. Watching them settling from spins on their rims, they wobble to their sides on the dirt, dirt she lifts her eyes from under her dark lashes. "Now the paper." He demands with an outstretched hand, as Lorelei lifts her eyes to the man from the coins. Handing it over calmly, she watches him snatch it. As he unrolls it, he sees the blank contents. "There is nothing written here." He turns. "What game do you play?" staring at the cream paper.

At once, Dimas has only a split second of seeing the tip of Lorelei's silver letter opener piercing the parchment as she stabs the tool through the paper into the man's throat. Dimas jerks, his mouth gaping with little sound but a gurgle. His body begins to convulse as he drops, the opener slipping out of him as he falls. Her expression of disgust holding on him as he takes his last breath, Lorelei flicks the blood off the silver makeshift weapon, the piece of parchment whipping off with a splatter of blood.

"I thought I was supposed to kill him?" Eber steps forward from the shadows of the back of the tent and slit his height cut into it.

She creeps her gaze over her shoulder. Her eyes set on him momentarily without any shroud of play or act, what show in them being the darker places her thoughts can go. In a blink, her nature shifts back to its stagecraft air. "Well, sometimes plans do not go as… planned." She scrunches her lips at her lack of a more clever speech.

He comes closer, looking over Dimas' body. "What matters is that it is done." She tosses the opener back to the little table, the sound a dull clatter on the wood. He passes his study over the coins on the ground. "Do not forget Dimas' pay."

The statement nips at Lorelei deep inside, lifting her focus from the dirty coins to him. "You think me such a desperate peasant that I would crawl on the ground for money." Her cold shade of blue eyes blends with her cold expression up at him. "I am not so lowly, Soldier."

Searching her, Eber tries finding something of her he would disrespect at this point. He looks over the blood on her hand from the killing of Dimas, her manner cool and unaffected, piercing eyes and how they hold on him as though she wishes to make him her next victim should he say another word. Lowering his gaze, Eber's study moves from her to the coins. Solemnly, he steps closer, taking a knee and picks up the coins, raising his hand and holding it out to her with the pieces in his palm. Her lips part gently, her gaze losing its coldness. She stares at Eber, his calm respect he hands to her without resentment, instead, looking into her eyes with a favor that she demands it.

She moves closer to him, Her expression fading from stunned to the warmer emotions that tingle her heart she has been trying to sort through up to now, surveying his face. "Eber," she whispers under her breath.

Of a sudden, yells from men and horses sound out in the camp. Lorelei jumps, her mind far enough away, her senses are genuinely frightened by the noises. Eber stands looking to the entry of the tent, when a burning arrow pierces through the roof, stabbing into the dirt. Lorelei lets out a shriek, lurching back from the incendiary. Surging towards the entry, Eber draws back the flap of the tent, seeing Krow at the ridgeline ordering the next round of attack. "Krow," Eber bites. "Lorelei!" He looks back to her, latching onto her wrist and yanking her along. She gawks, her wits still out of her as she hurries.

The next rain of burning arrows incoming, Eber ducts down at the back of a wagon loaded with hay, pulling Lorelei with him. The arrows dive into the hay, steadily igniting the dry fibers. Horses whinny, their cries desperate pleas to be free from their ties as the fires throughout the camp spread. They pull on the lines, their hooves churning the cold ground into the snow. Finally, the lines snap and the beasts flee for their lives, tearing through the camp, past men running for bows and arrows. The camp retaliates, firing arrows at the soldiers lining the ridge, another order to fire being shouted from Krow at his men. The soldiers draw back and let loose another downpour of fire.

Leaning back against the wheel of the wagon, Eber grits his teeth. "Damn him."

Coming out of her daze, Lorelei shakes her head. She looks up, seeing the growing flames in the bundle of hay. "Eber," she breathes.

Looking to where she is, he searches for the next destination in their path out. Seeing the fire spreading at the outskirts, their choices are few and are through the camp. "Come." He moves, Lorelei quick to follow.

The men in the camp yell to one another, ordering weapon supplies and attacks to defend. Some running with buckets of water, barking for help with the growing flames as the burning arrows land into supply tents. One of the men rallying the retaliation of arrows, spies Eber and Lorelei, his focus locking onto Eber's uniform. "A soldier!" he yells. A couple of men separate from the cluster.

Rushing Eber, the man draws his sword, swinging the weapon down at the captain. Having a moment to see the attack coming, Eber shoves Lorelei, getting the both of them clear as the blade clashes with the ground. Drawing Romhild, Eber slices down, cutting off the man's hands at the wrists, their grip still latched onto the handle of his sword. He yells in utter pain as Eber swings his longsword up, freeing the man's head from his body next.

Lorelei rolls to a hip, seeing the next man come at Eber. He lifts an axe, slashing at the Captain. Eber cuts at the man's weapon, slicing off the axe blade and grabbing the now empty stick the man is holding. With a yank, Eber pulls the man to him and onto Romhild, driving his sword through him. Her eyes captured by the waving light of fireballs raining from the sky, Lorelei calls out at the sight of falling incendiaries, "Eber!" Giving little choice, Lorelei rushes for the burning wagon, rolling under it as the arrows hit the ground. Using the dead man on Romhild, Eber blocks the fall of arrows at him, the flaming points stabbing into the dead man's back.

Dropping the man to the ground, Eber moves to pull Romhild free when a third and the largest man grabs at him. Wrapping a meaty arm around him, the man locks his hold around Eber's neck. The man draws a dagger, readying to stab when Eber grabs his hand, driving an elbow into the large man's side. The man lets out a pained growl as Eber jerks his arm, using the meaty appendage to pull the man where he wants him. Latching his arm around the man's neck, Eber takes hold of his head, snapping his neck. The large man drops limp in time for Eber to look up, finding the flames at the wagon spreading. Lorelei raises a hand, shielding her face from the flames she now is trapped by.

"Lorelei!"

Eber lifts to his feet, rushing forward when a portion of camp not far away, is hit by another rain of arrows. Burning points crash into the tent, some piercing the canvas and landing into the supplies inside. In a blink, Eber has the time to see the oil lamps resting inside, cases of oil being part of the supplies within. At once, the tent explodes. The blast sends him to his back on the ground, the shock wave across the ground launching snow into the air. The explosion of fire bursts over a huge part of the camp, engulfing all who stand near, including Lorelei, trapped by the wagon.

Rolling to a forearm, Eber starts to lift himself, the ringing in his ears giving way to horrifying screams of pain as men are burned alive in roaring flames. Steadily, Eber begins to hear Lorelei's cry lift to the sky in the mix.

KAPITEL XX

The last of the fires dying, Krow and his men move through the camp. "There look to be no survivors. Good," Krow says, a pleased smile sliding up one side of his face.

Cerny's nostrils flare with each breath of charred air, the scent of smoke heavy around him, his head bounces, the lack of Eber's scent what bothers the animal more. Tugging at the reins in Kalls hands, Cerny whips his head, leading Kalls to yank at the bit in the beast's mouth.

"Knock it off, you stupid animal!"

"I don't see him," Jorin says quietly.

"Who?"

"Eber," he bites.

"He is dead!" Kalls laughs at Jorin's needless worry. "Burned alive like the rest!" Surprising the man, Cerny bites at his uniform coat, yanking him to the ground. Rearing to his muscled back legs, Cerny kicks out his front hooves as Kalls looks up only to see Cerny slam down on him. Stabbing his sharp hooves, Cerny drives his powerful legs toward Kalls, trampling him into the muddy ground. His nostrils flare, cold breath puffing from them like smoke from a dragon's, his black mane swaying as he curves his neck, his dark eyes set forward at the group of soldiers.

"Demon horse!" Jorin peeps, his face turning whiter than the chunks of unmelted snow among the tinder of the camp.

"Do not let him get away." Krow looks back with a grin. "That horse is the best stock this rotten military has. He will have a new master." Krow sizes Cerny's worth. "He will suit me well." The steed snorts a cloud of hot breath.

A scent beginning to enter Cerny's deep nose, he tosses his head, arching his neck and lurching forward at a gallop. Nearly running over Jorin, the man jumps out of the way. "Lookout!" Krow and a few men lunge out of the way as Cerny tears past. His hooves pound into the mud, his pace slowing as Krow and Jorin's jaws drop seeing what the beast is running to. Slowly, Cerny trots to Eber, bouncing to a stop behind him. No greeting is returned from Eber to his horse as his focus and anger stay honed on Krow.

"You are alive?" Krow spouts woefully, seeing singed hems and soot covered fabric but little else wrong with the Captain. Slowly, Eber moves his hand towards the hilt of his blade. Vaguely seeing the younger man's movement, Krow looks to Eber's sword with his nearing hand, then up to his dark eyes. "You challenge me?"

"...I will kill you." The statement is said coldly and meant truly.

Starting forward, Eber quickens his pace, giving Krow little time to draw his sword as the two weapons clash, Krow's sliding off of Romhild. The men stay away, wondering how far any involvement on their part should go. Another clash of blades sends Krow's sword to a pile of burnt wood, lodging it in one of the pieces. With Eber lifting Romhild for his next strike, Krow yanks the blade free in time to block. The metals grinding on each other, the grading sound like a relentless honing block on the blades' edges. Gradually, with each hit, the Commander's sword chings until finally, the two men connect again with another slam of their blades against each other. Steadily, over the sounds of shaking crossguards, there comes the ping of a crack. Krow lowers his eyes from the Captain's to see that crack is forming in his own blade with Romhild pushing against the sharpened metal.

As though untouched, Romhild holds fast against Krow's sword as the man lifts his eyes back to Eber, a little more worry showing in them. With a kick to the Commander's middle, Eber forces the man to fall on his back to the ground. Seeing Eber lift his blade, the Commander's eyes flare and he pulls his sword over his chest as a last minute shield. Halting Romhild in his grasp and as he lets the blade fall to a stabbing position, the Captain drives the sword towards Krow, the weapon breaking through his blade shield, and stabbing into his body.

While jerking, Krow drops the other half of his sword still in his hand, his head falling to the ground and eyes staring into the sky. Steadying his breaths, Eber straightens, yanking Romhild from the dead man at his feet. Raising his angered eyes to the rest, Eber looks for the next challenge. The men look to one another as Jorin draws his sword. The rest of the soldiers follow suit and ready themselves to attack the solo man. Figuring this would be the way he dies, Eber turns the handle of his sword in his hand, simply waiting for all of them to come, eventually one of them surely to land a hit and bring an end to him.

From one of the small dying fires, the shadows waving on the ground begin to move out of sync with the flames, one of the shadows suddenly separating from the rest. Cerny stomps the ground, his head raising and nostrils flexing. Turning back the way of his horse, Eber watches the animal grow unnerved. The men halt, starting to sense danger themselves. At once, the shadows begin to grow, growls rising with them as Cerny jumps and nickers, the steed showing less resolve against whatever this is, than man.

One after another, more shadows jolt around the camp, growls and low roars following them. The men begin panicking at this witchery, Jorin barking to be ready for attack. Coming across his body, one of the shadows covers Jorin in its shade, the image of spreading claws over his face suddenly becoming real as they stab into his skin. Slashing the man to pieces, the shadow rushes to the ground quickly as it sprang from it. The men cry out to each other to be on alert, watching Jorin drop dead to the mud.

One after another, the shade creatures rise from the ground and dark corners of the rubbled camp, their shapes always shifting and morphing, growing fangs and claws, their mouths releasing growls that shake their jaws. The monsters surround the men, sweeping over the small army like a wave of roars, the cries of fear and pain spewing from the soldiers as they are slaughtered.

Each creature finishes its prey, lowering to the ground or clinging to the tattered remains of tents and wagons in the camp. Their jaws snap as they smack their mouths, the beasts of shade real enough to snarl at one another as blood drips from their fangs. With the shifting focus of one, the rest follow, turning towards Eber and Cerny. The steed shakes his head, anxiously moving behind Eber. Left to reevaluate the end of his life as he never would have seen coming, Eber stares at the creatures, gripping the hilt of his sword tightly. The monsters growl, their jaws shaking as they move forward towards him.

"Stop!" The shadow creatures halt, some nearly in range to touch Eber. Like a single mind, the entities look towards the command. Standing in her tattered clothes, ash on her skin, Lorelei pants. The creatures growl at her command. Seeing their defiance, Lorelei lifts her head, her bright eyes boring into the dark monsters. "Obey," she growls in return. Steadily, they bow their heads, lowering to the ground and recoiling slowly to the form of one shadow at her feet. Looking up from her bare feet in the mud and the shadow that rests in it, her resolve fades, her stern expression setting on Eber tiredly. Cerny nickers as Eber moves forward, coming before Lorelei. Confusion mixed with exhaustion, they study each other and what of her is left in the creature she now is, as the streams of smoke float into the air above them.

KAPITEL XXI

The streams of smoke float in the air as below them, the fire Koza made by the river, crackles and pieces of wood collapse in the pile of burning timber. Lorelei's eyes capture the glow of the flames as she stares into the fire and her memories.

Watching the fish on their sticks as they cook over the fire, Koza sits on a downed tree, his elbows on his knees and hands rubbing together as he likes to do. He looks up to the woman, her blue eyes encased by her heavy black lashes, a slow blink occasionally disrupting her stare at the flames. "I suppose they are ready to eat." Koza reaches for one of the skewers of fish. He surveys its cooked scales, approving. With a warm smile, he hands it over to her. She repays his politeness with her own warmth, taking it with a curl of her pink lips.

She studies the placement of her first bite, then takes it. "…Good," she nods.

Pleased, he moves to pick up his share and take part in his own enjoyment of the meal.

An hour or so later, the fire begins to smoke as it dies. From the burnt wood, the smoke scents the air. Resting his head against the tree which was his seat during the meal of fish, Koza lies with a bent arm for a pillow, his face loose and in sleep. Koza dreams whilst Lorelei lays tucked under her red shawl, asleep by the dwindling flames.

Carefully moving over the small pebbles of the river shore, brown booted feet sneak their way closer and closer to Koza. Gradually, the man draws a short sword, curving its blade ever so slowly round the front of Koza's throat. The motion is silent and soon to be deadly, until the man halts all movement, seeing a long blade starting to curve around his own throat. Darting out of the way, the man rolls to a stance, seeing Eber standing with drawn Romhild.

The man studies Eber, the commander seeming as silent and deadly as he was. Soon enough, Eber recognizes the man as the gypsy Lorelei insisted on helping. "Koza," he calls tamely to the sleeping captain.

Grumbling, Koza opens his eyes still half off in slumber, then sees where the call came from and who. At the sight of Eber standing somewhat over him, he jumps and clambers to his feet. "Sir?!" The motion stirs Lorelei, waking her for the unfolding event as well. Looking over the gypsy man, Koza turns back to Eber. "Was he... was he trying to?"

"Always sleep with an eye open, Koza." Eber pauses, glancing back to Lorelei. "Especially when the woman is up to something." Lorelei wrinkles her nose.

"Where are his two friends?"

At the coach, all is still and quiet. Cerny and the horses stand calmly dozing tied to a line of rope between two trees. Kasimir lies wrapped in a rich silk blanket lined with thick plush fur, meanwhile, Biagio rests in simple blankets and appears satisfied enough. Thayer sits with his back against one of the wheels of the carriage with his arms crossed off in sleep, as a subtle sound comes from the edge of the treeline.

The two gypsy men sneak noiselessly through the bushes and one points to the roof of the coach. "That's what we're after," The right one smiles as the left one follows the direction of his partner's finger.

The men make their way closer and as they round the coach they see the lone soldier's presence lit by the flames of the dying campfire. Though they are quiet, Cerny's other senses wake him, lifting his head to watch the men creep. They halt as they wait for a sign of the young man's consciousness. Convinced that he is fast asleep, one of them climbs the wagon and begins to lower chosen items to his comrade. After putting as much as could fit in the couple of sacks they brought, the one hops down silently from the roof and they aim to leave when at last minute the comrade sees the gold stool of Kasimir's, then snatching it they hurry off back into the woods with Cerny's head and ears following them.

Venturing deeper into the woods, the men slow their pace feeling free from any pursuit. "Haha!" the right man laughs. "Think of all we have! I can't wait to get to the nearest town to flaunt it all!" The man begins laughing again and is accompanied by his partner, then suddenly, a third laugh joins the cackle. The men stop dead in their tracks and look to each other.

"Who was that?" the right man asks.

"It wasn't me!" the left man answers.

"Well, it wasn't me!" the right man nips back.

Then between their heads, Ermanno leans. "And it sure wasn't me!"

At that moment, two hardy screams sound off from the woods. The shrieking yells only stirring those sleeping in the camp enough to roll over, Cerny sways his head back to the rope line, puffing a breath with a shake of his head which embodies Eber's own low level of tolerance for Ermanno.

Back at the river, the group stares off into the woods up the ridge as the screams fizzle out. At even pace with each other, Eber and Koza look to the woman. Blandly blinking a glance their way, she then turns her head more lively. "What?" She narrows her eyes. "I do not like the way you are glaring at me so accusatorially," she bites. Another scream flails from the woods, a gurgle tailing its end. The men keep their eyes on Lorelei. "Alright! So, perhaps I mentioned Kasimir's riches atop the coach, and perhaps I suggested these fine gentlemen fill their pockets with whatever the Holy Highness didn't need." She crosses her arms. "I hardly think any of that was the wrong thing to do." Her head aims away from the men.

"Koza," Eber names calmly.

"Yes Sir." He moves to a rush for the woods and the coach over the ridge and up the way.

"Looks like I won't have much from tonight," the gypsy man says, turning from the woods. "But I will have that sword of yours." His focus moves to Eber.

Her attention drifting to the two men still by the river, she watches the gypsy man prepare himself against Eber. For a moment there is quiet, the flowing river sweeping over and around rocks being the only sound. The gypsy man suddenly leaps toward Eber with blade ready to slash. Grabbing a fist full of the man's dark oversized shirt, Eber throws him into the mostly dead fire, sparks and ash plooming.

Lurching from the pit of burnt wood, the man pats a small flame igniting on his arm. With it frantically brushed out, the man glares up at Eber's dead expression. The gypsy man reaches for a chunk of burnt wood, throwing it at Eber for a distraction. In a vibration of air, Eber is gone and the wood keeps going, barely missing Lorelei's head. The man's eyes widen and mouth drops open when Eber rematerializes to his side, striking him with an arm. The harsh blow sends the man into the water of the river.

Lowering a frown, Lorelei grumbles, "That wood almost hit me in the face."

"...Almost."

"You think that is funny?"

The gypsy man crawls from the river, gasping. "Yes," Eber says blandly.

Disgusted, Lorelei continues her nips at Eber and his irritated watch of her. "Yes?" her tone lowers.

"You have caused troubles for me I did not need on this trip simply because you thought it would be... funny," he retorts, his pointed fangs emphasizing the last word.

Ceasing his coughing of water, the gypsy man looks up to Eber and Lorelei as they argue. "Do not speak to me like that, Soldier," the average fangs of a human in her mouth emphasizing the last word.

"I will speak to you as I wish, Woman," he says with a tone to suggest lowliness.

With the man gawking, Lorelei frowns deeply, a rumble starting to sound around her as Eber begins his own growl from low in his throat. Lorelei's eyes brighten as Eber begins to bare his fangs. The man stares at the two entities challenging each other and at once, he takes off up the shore of the river, running for the distant hills.

"I am going to scar that handsome face of yours, you Berin minion!" Her roar is joined by those of her shadows as they rise from the ground around her, their mouths opening wide with fangs, hands jerking open with claws.

His lip quivering over his fangs, Eber stands waiting for the creatures to come. At once, there is a sudden and vicious jerk in Eber's hand. The Commander looks down to his hand and witnesses the forceful movement as it happens again. Lorelei's scowl begins to slowly lesson as she realizes something is wrong.

"Rigor mortis," she whispers to herself, her glare of anger softening.

Over a moment, the jerking movements spread and pain becomes evident. Eber clutches his quivering hand to himself and attempts to force composure, then drops to a knee as his body is becoming uncontrollable. He bites his fangs together, the agony washing over his face.

Steadily, Lorelei's shadows lower to the ground, their growls turning silent as she stares at Eber's struggle.

Hearing his soft grunts of pain, her expression morphs to a quiet pity. She takes a step and another, coming closer to Eber, her zeal to fight with him faded away. She crouches to him, watching him bear the pain that bites at his body. Gently, she sets her hands to her knees, looking into his dark eyes full of torture. "Eber… I am sorry," her low voice gentles.

A moment passes and he replies between jerks. "As am I."

A soft smile unmeaning of any play or amusement warms her face and eyes on him. Quickly, she trains on where she is needed. She reaches for a smaller stick nearby, forcing it into his mouth as he bites down hard, his fangs digging into the wood and nearly snapping through as another wave of pain washes through him. Her hands set to his shoulders, trying to hold him in place as he begins to writhe, her empathetic gaze growing pained over him.

The carriage traveled the winding paths for three more days. The travelers now find themselves on the hillside road down to the village of Hieb. There is something foreboding in its quiet stillness, with no movement among the pale wooden buildings.

The setting sun's glow shines on the group as it makes its way into the village, then, it becomes clear why there are no gawking bystanders to greet the newcomers. On the muddy main road through Hieb, lie ashen bodies. Down side roads and alleyways lay more, men, women and children, on porches, in doorways and with them are horses, cattle and dogs all sharing the same fate. Pecked by vultures and scavenged by four legged predators, but whatever creatures were the cause of death were nothing belonging to Earth.

Among the dark brown mud and pale wood frames and bodies, the only rich color is in puddles by the dead and splashed on the walls of homes and wafting curtains from broken windows, it is the color red. Cautious and pitiful glances shift from place to place as the travelers continue through, bound for the church that's steeple bearing a long, slim cross that can be seen over the tattered rooftops.

The coach stops at the holy asylum's front door where Kasimir and Biagio disembark followed after a moment by Lorelei. After dismounting, Eber ties Cerny's reins onto the back of the coach and orders Thayer to find the livery and stable the horses. Koza fastens his horse and waves Thayer on and the carriage rattles as it goes. "Ermanno." The called steps forward to his Commander, Eber, who still feels the soreness in his body do to its further transformation from the rigor mortis. "Circle the perimeter of the village, if they return tell me."

The Second Lieutenant raises a brow, "They?"

"The soldiers that took our mortality, that made us untoten." Eber drifts his gaze over the devastation still not passing a glance to his men. "Their aftermath looked like this."

With a concerned breath, Koza asks, "You think it was the same untoten that attacked Hieb?"

"Possibly."

"Do you really believe they might come back?"

"As the Gypsy says, we are predators and predators always return to where they know they found food."

With a smile, Ermanno swings his battle axe free of its brown leather sheath like bindings on his back. "It sounds like we might have some fun tonight."

Ermanno makes his way out of sight as Kasimir and Biagio venture onto the yard of the church. As Kasimir reaches the door in a state of eagerness, he stops to consider the potential danger within. "Would it not be a good idea to have the protection of a soldier?" Kasimir barks back at Eber. The Commander turns his gaze to Koza who then steps from his leader's side and aims for the church door. He passes a brief glance to the wooden fence posts that signify the threshold of Holy ground. There's no feeling of fire in his blood, no sense of burning on his skin as he passes without harm. As Koza reaches Kasimir, the Head of the Church calls out to Eber again, "The more protection for me General, the better." The remark sends knowing stares from Koza and the Gypsy to Eber and unknowing glances from Kasimir and Biagio the same way. Eber lowers his eyes from Kasimir to the threshold in thought of what it means to set foot on Hallowed ground. Koza and Lorelei watch as Eber walks up to the fence posts, then with arms still folded and a slow motion he steps onto the Blessed dirt. The pain is slight and bearable and to all others unnoticeable. Eber takes his eyes from the ground and sets them once again on Kasimir. "How amazing you have not burst into flames," Kasimir chortles. Koza turns to the laughing man thinking the worst has happened and he knows of the Commander's damnation, then he realizes Kasimir jokes of the average damnation of a Der Vorfahr soldier and takes a relieving breath. "Open the door," Kasimir orders and Koza does so with Eber following up behind the Head of the Church and his devotee Biagio.

The smell of death rushes them as they enter the doorway into the nave lined with benches. The low clerestories let in the light of the setting sun, thereby giving sight to the scene. More people dead, some embraced by another in a last comfort. Here, there is a difference though. "There's no blood," Koza notes.

As Kasimir weaves through the bodies without a Blessing, Eber moves up beside Koza, "Apparently there were none among the undead that attacked who could walk unharmed on Hallowed ground as you do."

"Or tolerate it as you do," Koza retorts. "These poor people."

"Do not pity their choice."

Koza looks to Eber, "choice?"

"To starve," the General meets the Captain's gaze. "Than be eaten."

"Search all the rooms," Kasimir's plea to Biagio is heard and Eber turns to follow, curious of what greedy desire has brought them all here.

Outside of the church Lorelei pans over the wholesome imagery of humanity's devotion to God in the fence bordering the holy ground and the cross atop the steeple. Letting out a sigh, she turns from the sight. "I could use a drink," heading back to the tavern seen earlier as they entered Hieb.

Searching in benches and sacristies, Biagio digs, carelessly tossing things to the side. Kasimir opens the door to a private room and enters hastily. The body of a bishop rests in a chair behind a large desk with papers scattered. Eber steps into the doorframe after Biagio follows the path of his leader. Koza watches over Eber's shoulder with disdain as Kasimir roughly moves the bishop's body aside. While Kasimir takes to pulling open drawers to the desk, Biagio kneels at a trunk and lifts the heavy lid. "Here it is!" The overseeing soldiers' eyes drop from the Holy Highness to Biagio. Kasimir looks up to see his follower holding up a bundle of cloth.

Biagio sets the bundle in Kasimir's waiting hands. "Wonderful." The Holy Man's eyes gleam with his own revelation as he pulls at the fabric revealing a stone the size of a man's head. In it is the vague impression of what looks to be a bare foot print.

"What is it?" Koza ponders.

The Commander states blandly, "Don't ask questions, you won't receive truths."

With a cock of his head Kasimir smirks and walks up to the General. "You call me a liar? You call me a sinner?"

With beads of straining stamina forming on his face Eber replies wearily, "It is a mockery for both of us to be within these walls and not burn." Standing with his arm against the door frame above his head, Koza shifts his gaze from his Commander to Kasimir with a restrained smirk at the conviction.

After a pause, Kasimir begins to notice the wear on Eber's face. "Is something the matter General?" Koza looks back to Eber seeing for himself how the time on Holy ground is taking its toll. The Commander's reply to Kasimir is nothing but a dead stare sending him to boredom. "I don't need you," the Holy Man lifts his nose and turns back to the desk. "Leave now."

Koza steps to the side allowing Eber to pass. As Eber moves down the aisle his pace seems to slow, then of a sudden he stumbles and sets a steadying hand on one of the pews. Koza shoots a glance back to the room where Kasimir and Biagio reside to see that they are remaining unaware. The bracing hand begins to burn on the Holy furniture and Eber lifts it to see his palm is seared and is not healing, but spreading.

Over his shoulder, he sees Koza approaching with concern and halts him with a raised subtle hand that demands solitude. Koza stops and stays back as Eber looks to the door knowing that the time of voluntary movement is running out.

He makes his way through the front door and looks up from the few steps before him to the threshold a short walk away. The difficulty of moving his legs increases as he goes down the steps and starts for the open gate of the fence. With another haggard misstep he stumbles again, but this time drops to a knee. Holding his burning hand to him in pain he stares at the threshold as if it were a cool river in a roaring blaze. Forcing himself to stand, he finally makes it through the gate, leaving the Hallowed ground.

He drops to the dirt on his knee. Thinking the pain would be gone once free of the holy land, Eber is met with even more. Raising his hand, the scars are still there, the burning still flooding through his body. Panting a little, his fangs click each other as his jaws come together slightly with each pass of breath in and out. He lifts his eyes from his wounds, looking down the street for the tavern as the dark clouds above begin to spit rain.

KAPITEL XXIII

Lorelei stands at the bar of the tavern Inn, uncorking a dusty bottle. Picking up a glass from the drying rack, she eyes it over, finding a spot of dirt. Moving her tongue, she spits into the glass, wiping it out with the cuff of her oversized white shirt. Eyeing it again, she is satisfied and begins to pour herself a drink.

Hearing the creaks of wood, she listens to whomever is coming up the steps of the tavern. Passing a glance over her shoulder at the sound of the door opening, she spies Eber and grows a smirk looking back to the booze. Lifting her glass, she turns. "Join me in a drink?" Watching him, her smile holds until she focuses more on his eyes, her hand lowering the glass. His onyx spheres stare at her with a slow growing life to them. It is a life of something that wishes to take hers. Lorelei stiffens, beginning to sense it is not Eber she looks upon in the moment, but his hunger.

At once, Eber moves forward. "Eber." She tries reminding the mindless. His quick steps bring him ever closer to her. "Eber." Lorelei steps back, the soldier's presence forcing an instinctive response from her as he reaches her, her back hitting the edge of the bar as she dips her head back from his, coming towards her. His snarl, his lifting lips slowly begin to lower back over his fangs, his dark eyes staring into hers starting to regain the mind behind them. Gradually, his eyes lower, finding her hand on Romhild. Her worried gaze follows his, seeing her fingers wrapped around the sword at his side. Looking back up to him, she begins to see the changes on his face as other times her touch has brushed across the blade. Steadily, the usual calm Eber returns.

"I am not healing like before." Raising his hand, he stretches the burnt skin over his palm as she looks at it, seeing the marks of God's renouncing of the soldier in the wounds to the bone.

Watching him change, Lorelei recognizes the manner of a man from long ago, responding with a gentleness from a woman long ago, "I am sure you were hungry after you underwent rigor mortis, now that you endured holy ground, you are starving," a pity sounding in her deep voice of velvet. Feeling the truth of her words burn his throat, the pain of his body becomes second thought, drifting behind the sound of blood moving under the woman's skin. The smell of her skin, the smell of that blood, it shows him the minds of a wulf, of a mountain cat, how they do not smell the deer; they smell the meat on its bones, they do not smell the blood; they taste the life of the prey as it drains away.

Pausing, that pity surveys him, then sets her glass of liquor to the bar with a sigh. Bringing her hand back between them, she turns her wrist up to him, growing a smile. "Join me in a drink?" She wonders at his thoughts as he carefully examines the soft meat she holds up for him to taste. "What is the matter, Soldier?… Do you not like the idea of biting me?" she plays. The lift of his eyes to hers lowers her curled lips. Among the aches in his body, the familiar one in his chest grows the longer his eyes linger in hers. Wanting things to be simpler, wanting thoughts of the past to stay there, she lifts another smile, regaining her play. "How do you know I would not like it?" She archs a brow.

Gradually, the corner of Eber's mouth curls when he turns her wrist over, setting her hand back to Romhild's hilt. His hands grip onto her sides, his fingers tipped by short claws tugging and poking through her wrinkles of fabric. He glides to her hips, guiding her to the nearby table, the back of her legs hitting the wood, his body pinning her there. Under her skin, her blood warms as it rushes through her body, blood which he can smell, making his lips part over his fangs.

Yanking at her layers of skirt, Eber's hold changes and he roughly hoists her to the surface by her thighs. He leans to her, his mouth latching onto her neck, forcing her head to one side, her long wavy coal hair bunching on her shoulder, his body pushing her down to the table as he comes over her.

Her shining blue eyes close pleasurably, her lower tone releasing a throaty breath as his mouth shifts on her neck, moving his deep bite to another tender spot under her jaw. His instincts commanding his needs with his claws piercing into her skin, his fangs burying further into her throat, tipping her head back. At the same time, the commands of her instincts glide her hand over his chest, pushing at his coat, while the other stays locked on Romhild, her legs wrapping around him.

"...You taste sweet," he says hoarsely, his mouth moving once again. "…You have always tasted sweet."

The tugging of his clothes not pulling him flush enough against her, Lorelei's hand reaches from the rim of his coat up his shoulder and neck, into the wavy locks of his black hair. Her fingers curl in the strands, securing him to her, another low timbered breath from deep in her chest brushing his ear.

The approaching night makes everything in the village more dismal as the group carries on about their business. Koza's business being that of watching Kasimir's, Thayer taking care of the horses with water and food, then there's Ermanno. The bald man patrols the edge of the village in search of any threats. As he swings his axe in sadistic play at the low branches of helpless trees, he suddenly halts and stares off into the woods. Like a deer catching the scent of a predator or a predator catching the scent of the deer, Ermanno raises his nose to the air and takes two short sniffs followed by a long one. His head lowers and the corner of his mouth lifts to an eager grin as he heads off back to the village.

The tavern Inn sets dark with little sound, say for Lorelei's soft breaths while she brushes her face against the side of Eber's head, their strands of black tangling. He sits on one of the chairs at the table with her sat on him, her layers of skirt are tucked up to her thighs with legs straddling his lap.

His mouth is loosely on her throat, his hunger satisfied, he satisfies other hungers now. Her mind cloudy from entanglement atop the table, the thinning of her blood also hazes her thoughts, her head setting against his as her eyes close and lips separate. The mist in her head actually making thought easier as it simplifies, Lorelei's soft breaths turn to softly spoken words, the guise of lust removing its mask as something more pure than expected in the moment.

"...Eber," she whispers against him. "...I love you." Her grip on Romhild's hilt tightens. The sudden grunt and smack to the wooden steps outside snapping her attention, Lorelei looks to the tavern door as it slams open. Less reactive, Eber looks to see Ermanno barging in.

"Commander!" Ermanno spouts with excitement, then halts. Seeing them in a more private moment, Ermanno blinks between him and the woman. "Never mind me!" He grabs a chair, turning it and planting himself with arms on its back, setting his chin in one of his palms. "Please, keep doing it." He grins his crooked smile. Her lips straight, Lorelei's aura begins to growl.

Flying through the air out the door, Ermanno lands in the street with a slide through the mud, the shadow creature letting out a snort through its growl of pointy teeth. Bending to the boardwalk of the tavern, the shadow lowers and returns through the door past Eber coming out.

"What is it, Ermanno?"

Lifting himself up from the mud, he spits out the gunk and shakes it from his face, the rain starting to wash it free from his bald head. With Lorelei coming out of the tavern to stand by Eber, her expression of little tolerance gives the Lemure soldier another smirk. "The undead are coming back." The joy in his dark eyes flares.

Lowering his head, Eber's line of sight holds with Ermanno's until a leisurely blink moves it over the Woman. In a few steady breaths, their expressions share a conversation. His, a solid stare that gleans a thinking mind, while hers turns to a smirk which shows her own twinkle of thought. "What a surprise this will be for Kasimir." She turns for the Inn.

Vaguely watching her go, Eber's focus moves into the street as he comes down the steps. "Show me where."

"Of course." He stands and gives one hardy flick of mud off his arms, then disappears into a vibration of air with Eber soon after him.

Strigoi – Of Romanian origin. Derived from the Romanian verb striga "scream", this blood lusting creature is known to tear horrific screams from its victims before their deaths. They are thought of as troubled souls and in some fables are even mentioned to be living people with particular magical properties. It was often thought that Strigoi were beings with two hearts and therefore two souls.

Finally sickened enough by the smell of death in the church, Koza steps outside where death is still present, but at least the scent of it is swept away by the cool night air. With Kasimir lending no hint of his plans to clarify Koza's purpose to continue watching him, he ventures to explore the village, perhaps there are survivors. A peek in a window here and there and a glance inside an open door every so often reveals no sign of living or living dead. The young Captain walks up onto a warped and slanted wooden porch and moves towards an open front door. As he steps into the doorway the light of the clouded moon shines down on a poorly made doll with shredded straw hair and a piece of pink cloth for a dress. Its craftsmanship is inexpert, but that merely tells Koza more about it. He considers its creator, how it was most likely a mother making do with the materials she could afford and how the odds were that the little girl who owned it loved it as though she could want for no better. Everything in the village is quiet, easily allowing for a moment of silence for those souls whose history of existence has culminated to a simple doll lying on a floor.

With victory literally in hand, Kasimir departs from the church with a firm grip on the once more covered stone. Kasimir and Biagio make their way down the main street through Hieb, eager to find the General and leave for Loviturä. After a few minutes they catch sight of the tavern.

Stepping up in through the door of the tavern, Kasimir and Biagio are greeted by the sight of Lorelei pouring herself a drink, with her back to the men. Paying little mind to her, Biagio watches Kasimir near her. Setting the stone down on the bar, Lorelei's eyes glide over to the object as the cloth its wrapped in flops down a corner, showing a glimpse of the rock. She looks back to her drink.

"What are you having?" Kasimir smiles.

"Vodka."

"Not a bad choice." He takes the bottle, her sideways gaze watching him put the bottle's rim to his lips.

Her brows lift and she goes back to her glass, taking a sip. "Used to the strong stuff I see."

The butt of the bottle sets to the bar and Kasimir smirks. "This is a celebration, Gypsy."

"Mmm, good for you." She swigs, tilting her head back.

Her dismissive nature towards the old man not bothering him, the motion of her drinking from the glass does. He sees bite marks on her neck when her head straightens and hair falls back around her face. Kasimir's study of those marks hangs on her throat through the thick hair, his eyes narrowing the more his mind reasons their existence.

Lightly, Kasimir lifts his free hand and brushes a stroke of her hair over her shoulder. In a blink, Lorelei latches a tight grip around his wrist, her shining eyes turning to him, a darkness in their brightness. "…You have been bitten, woman." Her solid gaze gives no reply. "You think I do not recognize such bites?… You think I do not know who has put them there?" He chuckles. "I have always thought him one of Hell's rodents, I see he has transformed completely."

At once, Lorelei's deathly serious glare into Kasimir's tarnished soul shifts to light humor. "Who?" she asks with the innocence of a child, fluttering her dark lashes.

Kasimir gives another soft laugh. "There is only one man whose mouth you would let on your body." Growing a smirk, Kasimir grows one of his own. "Your filthy body." Her smirk lowers just as slowly as it lifted. Around her grows a growl, sounds that call Biagio's attention to the tug of his coat, readying to grab at his daggers. He looks around the tavern as the walls creak, the tables and chairs beginning to quake and liquor bottles starting to rattle. Having a better idea than most of what is coming the brighter Lorelei's eyes shine their blue, Kasimir reacts. He grabs at her glass of vodka, tossing its remains into her face. The liquid burns the moment it touches her tissue, her eyes slamming shut as she grabs at her face, letting out a pained howling scream.

"Mikhail?" Koza turns from the doll to the familiar soft voice. Thayer looks over Koza's unique sullen frown. "Are you alright?"

Without answer to his question, Koza replies, "did you take care of the horses?"

"Yes, they are watered and fed." Koza nods while shifting his eyes to the boards under his feet. "What became of Kasimir?" his young friend asks.

"He did not come here to help these people. He came here for a stone."

"A stone?! Why on earth a stone?"

"I don't know." Suddenly from within the core of the village a woman's scream rings out. Koza and Thayer look off the porch of the old house in wonder of the painful cry. Koza steps forward as he recognizes the voice.

Standing at the edge of the village, Ermanno sniffs the air, Eber folding his arms and watching the Lieutenant as he gleefully explains. "Can you smell them?" he asks the Commander who stares back at him blankly. "I can." He turns to the woods. "If I stretch my senses I can even hear them a little." he grins, "They are coming quickly."

Looking to the woods, Eber holds his focus and gradually the look reaches through the forest. They are unhoned skills, but he too can smell them, sense them, hear them. He can hear their sounds of rushing through brush, their grunts and growls at each other like a pack of animals communicating as primitive nature. He can hear their cries, their screams when another scream of one who is alive rings through his senses. His eyes shift abruptly from their dead examination of the forest, to a glare of the village which had been behind him.

"That sounded like the woman," Ermanno tilts his head back, far less concern trickling over the homesteads below as Eber lowers his expression darkly and disappears in a pulse of air. Watching the Commander's haste to respond and show of unhappiness, Ermanno crosses his arms over his broad chest. "Heh, I have a feeling that someone is getting stabbed." He vanishes in the same pulse of air after Eber.

Koza rushes up to the tavern steps following the trail of the holler. Thayer comes up beside him with the Captain crashing through the door only to halt immediately.

A shady figure of snarling lips and bared teeth crushes down on a table, smashing its claws into the wood while another shadow beast growls and slams to the wall as though not seeing the boundary.

Hitting the floor from the chaos, Kasimir lifts himself to an elbow as Biagio rushes to him. Grabbing at the old man's arm, the devotee helps him up. "She is the host of those demons, if she is blind, then as are they." At that, Lorelei's head whips to the men with her shadows' heads jerking to do the same, their eyes open wide whilst hers stay shut tightly in pain.

"But she is not deaf." Biagio yanks Kasimir out of the way, Koza doing the same for Thayer as the shade monsters crush the floorboards where the men stood.

Steadying himself, Biagio flaps his coat to the side, clutching a dagger and drawing it from its hidden place. Taking his brief moment of aim, he flings the weapon for the Woman's head. Covering the distance of the room in a blink, the dagger meets a sudden halt in Eber's grip, the Commander having crossed the distance of the village in the same blink. Holding the sharp point at his chest, Eber looks from the weapon, up to Biagio. In another wave of air, Eber moves to the front of Biagio, the man having only the time to vaguely see the soldier before Eber shoves his hand against the man's chest with force to send him out the door, into the street with a grunt and thud.

The sound of movement alerting Lorelei once more, her focus shifts to where Eber stands in the room, her shadow beast training on the same spot. Growling and snarling, the creatures rush the spot, fangs bared and claws drawn, honed to cut and slice. "Lorelei," Eber calls softly. Her own snarl drops from her face, the beasts lurching to a sudden stop nearly at the soldier. As her expression softens, now knowing who her target was in that moment, the shadows' fangs fade and claws draw in. The ridges of the figures in feral jaggedness smooth, the Soldier not their prey.

Coming down the steps, Eber halts with a boot still on a step above, watching Biagio as the man pushes himself up from the ground. Walking to the overhang of the tavern, Kasimir comes to the untoter's back. "Eber Soldat, a vampiric monster... Sounds right."

Idly, the Nachzehrer Commander speaks. "The undead that slaughtered this village are returning. They will be here in moments." Biagio stands, jumping his shock to Kasimir who stares at the bland eyes of Eber as he turns the Holy Highness's way up the steps. Age and fear forcing haggard breath in and out of his body, Kasimir holds panic on his face. "The church… It will protect you from them… and me." Kasimir taking his last words seriously, he sees the history of disfavor in the reflection of those black eyes that stare so coldly. "Run." The simple command is heeded with passion as Kasimir clutches at his robes and runs with stone in hand for the old building of salvation. Watching the man flee, Biagio sprints after him.

"I can chase?" Ermanno steps up, grinning, the farm cat watching the little mice running.

"…No." The mountain cat watching the little mice for the tiny morsels they are to him.

"Madam Zima!" Koza rushes to the woman, sloshing the bucket of water as he sets a bowl to the bar. "Here, wash out your eyes." Pouring the water, he sets the bowl in her hands. Splashing it in her eyes, Lorelei begins to feel the relief of the water. Gently setting a wide hand to her back, Koza shows his pity for her whilst she wipes at her eyes. The click of boots on the wooden floor drawing his attention from her, he looks to Eber and Ermanno.

"Thayer," Eber halts, the young man's focus whipping to the calm call. "Let the horses loose."

Glancing to Koza from the confusion, the Captain and old friend simply stares back. "Yes Sir," Thayer gives a bow of the head and scurries off.

"What now?"

Looking to Koza, more the woman he is comforting, Eber replies, "the untoten are coming back to Hieb."

"What?!" Koza faces him more squarely. "What are we to do?"

Eber folds his arms, his posture of a seemingly pained chest returning as he thinks. "…Nothing."

"We do not need to worry about combat?"

"There is no reason to fight them." Eber lifts his thoughts from the woman to the man in front of him, to his mossy green eyes of disarray. "Do you forget, Koza?... We are now monsters too." Unable to argue, Koza blinks, his breaths expanding his broad chest, his still very human muscle and warm skin tone not a good reminder of what lurks inside.

Massaging her aching eyes, Lorelei stands, peeking her lids open enough to see the destruction her shadows have caused in the tavern. There comes a small moment of quiet as Koza watches Eber, gradually seeing how the man is looking at the woman. His eyes are cold, but within the onyx pits there is something almost trying to climb out. It is care. From the depths of his inhumanity, he cares about her pain.

"Are you alright?" Eber asks Lorelei, his body and manner remaining distant while his voice reaches, seemingly against his nature.

Blinking her eyes open, they squint and still have redness to them. "I am fine," she nearly growls, not so taken aback by his unusual care, but seeming to hate it in this moment.

Koza stays silent, trying to hide himself at the edge of their interaction. The young Captain's experiences with Eber have molded his idea of the man as emotionless, yet these moments with the woman, with Lorelei show times when emotion is not so strange for him, making it all strange to Koza.

Shortly, Thayer comes across the street, hopping up the steps of the tavern and youthfully bouncing in the door. "Commander." He nears Eber as the man stands in the window, eyes calmly surveying the church in the distance. "I let the horses go. Yours nearly ran me down wanting to get free."

"Cerny can smell them coming."

Lifting his chin, Thayer nods vaguely. "Aw... Who is them?"

"It's the undead that killed the people in this village, Johan." Koza straightens his back, the now empty bucket clanging to his thigh. "They are coming back."

"And we are staying here?" he asks nervously.

Passing a glance over Eber, Koza looks back to the younger soldier. "Evidently."

Inside the church, in front of the ambo, Kasimir clutches his precious rock to his chest. "I was a fool!" he grumbles. "I should have known better than to allow my transport to be led by Soldat!" He turns and passes back. "That man would not be of help to me. Of course he would delight in my death."

"You are Ambrozij Kasimir, the Head of the Church, the holiest of power under God himself. Why would a soldier of Berin's be at odds with you?" Biagio says, sitting on a pew, his elbow resting atop a raised knee.

"God," Kasimir chortles. Biagio curves his brows, the man's snicker at the highest power not something he expects laughter at. "In Der Vorfahr, I am God." Mild surprise crosses the follower's face as Kasimir defines his deeper thoughts. "Soldat is the Devil."

KAPITEL XXV

Preta – Of Indian origin. Said to be invisible, there are tales of Pretas being seen by people in certain mental states. They are described as being human looking with emaciated bodies and mummified skin. As added agony, it is mentioned that the moon can burn them while the sun can freeze them. The Preta is believed to be a greedy person in life whom fate inflicts with insatiable hunger in death. Whether it is riches or life's crimson fluid, the Preta spends eternity craving for it, giving its kind the generic name of "hungry ghosts".

A drip of rain from the darkening sky falls to the wet ground near the church. Another drop leading a rush of water as it starts pouring from the Heavens above.

A dull leather boot pressing into the wet mud, a man sways to a stop, his jerking figure halts at the edges of the church yard. When the creature sniffs through the rain drops at the church, another unsteady being comes closer. Sensing the creature's closeness, the first untoter curls its lips over its fangs letting out a loud growl the other reacts to with its own.

Slowly, their glossed eyes staring at the house of God with the scent of life inside it. More and more undead begin to show, their focus on the same smell of blood from the dead man with more snarls and low roars ringing out as more and more untoten flood through Hieb.

Outside the tavern, the first signs of the creatures in the village pass by the window Koza stands looking out of. He watches them spread through the streets, atop the buildings, down alleyways. Letting out a breath, Koza looks down from the sight. One of them comes close by the window, moving along down the boardwalk, bringing a scowl to Koza's brow. The creature doesn't look familiar, but what it wears does. The mangled face tattered by a harsh death. Koza turns to Ermanno and Thayer sitting miscellaneously at a table towards the front. "You were right, Sir, they are the undead soldiers who killed us in the mountains."

Eber sits at the table nearest the bar, leisurely rapping his fingers on the surface, not needing confirmation of his assumptions.

"They've moved across the land like a plague," Thayer says, fiddling with one of his close range daggers.

"How are we going to kill all of them?" Ermanno sits with hands between his knees, hunched over on the chair.

"Sir?" Koza asks, twisting his torso Eber's way.

The sound growing on her nerves, Lorelei stares at the raps of Eber's fingers whilst he answers the captain. "We will not." The men turn the way of the commander. "We will use them." They listen as Eber finally voices his thoughts. "These creatures seek living blood, not ours."

"So we could just walk out of here, down the main street at our leisure and get away without a fight with a single one of them?" Ermanno nods, glancing to Koza. "That is somewhat disappointing," slanting his lips.

"Yes." Eber raps on the table, Lorelei's focus still trained on the noise.

"Then let's go!" Thayer chirps happily, his young voice sounding of youth's ignorance as ever.

"We are not leaving." Thayer's delighted grin drops at the Commander's dead reply.

As Eber opens his mouth to add, he raps again, Lorelei's reddened eyes lifting to his. "Rap them one more time and I cut them off." He looks to her, her face lined with exhaustion, pain, and no patience.

His fingers aimed upward to come down in another rhythm, he lowers his hand flat to the table. "…How long do you think Berin will let us live as those things out there?" Koza glances over his shoulder out the window at the creatures with the same hungers as his fellow soldiers. "Berin loves power, to have inhuman soldiers with our inhuman strengths he would adore. However, if Kasimir dies the entire city of Loviturä will only see us as monsters, not powerful protectors. Without Kasimir to calm the public, Berin will face an uprising like no other, one he is not willing to lose wealth or resources over. He will have us killed to quell the riots." Eber looks to Koza. "No, we are not leaving without Kasimir."

"But will he not demand our deaths, much as his followers?" Koza questions.

"...Yes, until he needs us." Koza begins seeing the parts of a plan Eber has been making since arriving in Hieb. "...The undead in the streets will starve, but so will Kasimir, and eventually." Eber's eyes shift back ahead of him over the table. "The Holy Man will be willing to deal with the Devil."

"You are the Devil?" Ermanno chuckles, lifting his lips over his crooked fangs, finding far more amusement out of Eber's remark then meant.

Brushing off the bald man's taste in humor, Koza crosses his arms over his broad chest. "And how would we get him out of Hieb without being attacked by the undead?"

In a slow blink, Eber trains on Lorelei. Rubbing at a temple, she feels his eyes on her and looks up, glancing about the room which is now focused on her. Shifting her skirts, she takes one leg off the other she had crossed, reaching down to the side of her chair. "The same as what hid your scents to the horses." She hoists a ribbon of vine from her travel bag. "Wire Vine." Pulling back her oversized sleeve, she smiles at Koza, exposing the weed wrapped around her arm. "What do you think has hidden the scent of my blood from them so far?" Hesitantly, Koza's gaze shifts, trying to hide what he is thinking. She chuckles. "You think they do not smell me because I am a monster too?" She lowers her eyes to the table. "Perhaps." Her smile softens. "Either way, the wire vine will hide the scent of the Holy Highness."

Two days later, night drips into day as the thunderstorm continues overhead, filling the daytime sky with dark clouds. Pouring rain splashes the puddles of blood on the streets and spreads the red color further around Hieb.

The small church in sight a few tattered homes away, Eber watches from a rooftop, his posture crouched with arms over his bent knees while staring through the drips of rain, locked on the house of God, of Kasimir, water directing lines of hair in his face.

"Koza?" the young captain turns up to Thayer, leaning back a bit in his seat under a narrow overhang of the roof. "I am so hungry." Thayer grips his knees in his arms, sitting up the way on the rooftop under the overhang of the second story.

Pity on his face, Koza frowns. "I am sorry my friend. It will not be much longer." Thayer looks to Eber. "The Commander has his plans for Kasimir."

"What do you think goes through the Commander's mind when he is like this, quiet I mean?"

Examining the General the few buildings away from them, he passes his answer to the Lieutenant. "Do not invest much effort in trying to understand the Commander, Johan." The men turn back the way of the leader. Smoothly in that moment, Eber rises to a stance and in a vibration of air, disappears. Koza and Thayer look to each other, then follow after.

Picking a small piece from the chunk of bread, Lorelei avoids the moldy areas on the loaf, putting the bite in her mouth. "So, you gypsies make bargains, yes?" Ermanno comes to a lean on the edge of the bar where the woman stands. Shifting her gaze to him with a jerk of her heavy brows, she puts another bite between her lips.

"Yes." The answer spitting out crumbs that Ermanno watches fall.

"How would you like to make a bargain?" he grins.

Swallowing, "What sort of bargain?" she asks, not enthralled to hear his stipulations.

"Well, I was thinking, I am hungry, starving." His dark eyes flare as his sharp teeth grit the word. "Thirsty for human blood, and you are a human." She stares at him unblinking, patience not on her waiting expression. "So here is my bargain, you let me have some of your blood, just a little." He puts a finger to his thumb to show the small amount, his claws clicking together. "And I will bed you." He grins.

"...You are offering me sex with you as a payment?" She stares.

"Yes."

"That I would want?"

"Yes." Waving a hand, he continues. "Being so freakish as you are, I imagine even the bravest man has feared to touch you... It is out of pity really."

"..." With an abrupt growl, shadows tear from the floor under her, biting onto Ermanno and crashing him out the front door. Flying through it once more, Ermanno lands in the street with a slide through the mud as before. The shadow lets out a snort through its growl of pointy teeth, lowering back to the ground and returning back up the steps and in the door.

Letting out a sigh, she turns back to the bar, snatching up an apple among the foods Koza had found for her. "Gypsy." The familiar summons draws her mid bite of the apple. Coming up to her, Eber's focus sets solely on her, ignoring Ermanno's grunts outside the tavern inn.

"What is it, Soldier?"

"I need something of you." His dead eyes hold down on hers. Growing a smirk, she bats at a buckle of his black uniform coat. "My body?" she plays.

"No."

Her play drops to an immediate scowling pout. "Very well, what do you need from me?"

"Something you will enjoy just as much." The promise lifting her mood, the smirk returns.

As nightfall had arrived, the stormy clouds of thunder held fast overhead. Biagio sits with a hand pressing on his stomach to try and quiet the sounds of hunger. Kasimir rests on the floor against a wall still holding his precious stone. "We must outlast these creatures."

Suddenly, they hear the crisp sound of a bite into an apple. The taste of its sweet juice and crunchy flesh floods their memories. They both turn to the sound as Lorelei steps into view from a back way into the church. "Ah, but will you outlast Commander Soldat and his men?"

Kasimir climbs to his feet to stare at the Woman while Biagio mainly stares at the fruit. "What do you want creature? Why has he sent you here?"

She turns the apple in her hand to find another unblemished, perfectly ripe spot to sink her teeth. "I am sure you are tired of this place, as is Eber, but he is not starving like you. I am here to barter an agreement."

"What agreement?" he asks as Biagio steps up closer by him, still focused on what's in the Woman's hand.

She takes another juice filled bite that reminds the men not only of their hunger, but their thirst as well. "I am sure you wonder how I was able to walk among the undead and not be attacked." She raises her other hand to play with wire vine wrapped around her forearm. "Wire vine is the means you need to get out of this village alive, so long as you follow Eber's plans to ensure he and his men are accepted by Loviturä's citizens with open arms."

"You want me," he grumbles. "The Head of the Church, to approve of your demon lover and his henchmen?"

She narrows her gaze and spreads her smile. "You have lowered your beliefs for far pettier things." Kasimir burns with hate for her. "This egotistical decision Kasimir, will mean your life. Make it wisely, not rashly."

Biagio takes a step forward towards the food in her hand and the look in his eye is one of dangerous desperation. Harming a woman for a bite to eat doesn't seem all that wrong to him now. Lorelei's smile doesn't shrink and the blue of her eyes is turning brighter the closer he gets. "Biagio!" Kasimir calls to stop him from advancing. The man turns and looks. "Do not." Kasimir keeps his gaze on the shining blue of hers.

"Weigh your options," she suggests, then turns to leave as she sinks another bite into the apple.

Leaving through the front door of the church, the Gypsy passes by untoten without incident, proving to Kasimir that there is a way to get out alive, but only if he agrees to Eber's bargain. At a mark of ten or so paces away from the gate to the church grounds, Lorelei lets go of the apple dropping it as if she had no more wish to eat on it. After she disappears from view, the men in the church watch the apple closely.

KAPITEL XXVI

Another wet day passes and every undead is accounted for, but things have become more stagnant. It seems apparent that as long as there is the smell of life inside the church, the untoten have no intention of leaving.

The juicy apple sets in the mud past the gate of the church fence. Staring at the fruit through a window, Biagio tastes the food in his dry, hungry mouth, the bit of mud on it nothing to ruin its flavor. "What are we going to do?" He blinks from the food to Kasimir, pain on his face.

"What do you mean 'what are we going to do?'… I will not give in to that creature. Agree to Soldat's terms?!"

"We are going to die here."

"No we are not." Kasimir turns in his seat, shifting his robes as he crosses his legs. "The undead will go away." He waves a hand, his trumpet sleeve swaying.

"No! They can smell us! They are not leaving!" He looks to the pews that once held the dead bodies. "The people who ran to this place before, thought they might go away!" Having no favor for the sharp replies, Kasimir glares at Biagio. "There are thousands who are closer to God than thou, but still, you are the Head of the Church, can you not do something against Hell's rodents?!" he bites his teeth together. Kasimir lowers his brows to a glower, his lips tightly together. Giving a one breath chuckle, Biagio answers his own conjecture. "No… Of course you can't." With a snarl, Kasimir watches Biagio draw out his daggers and aim for the door.

Opening the church door, Biagio makes his way slowly out of the building. With care and focus on the untoten around the area, he treks down the stone path to the white gate at the property's border. Carefully, Biagio ventures closer to the fruit. Taking a heavy breath, he lifts his booted foot over the church's threshold, stepping off of Hallowed ground. Quickly he checks the places of distant undead, finding them fighting among themselves or wandering aimlessly away from the immediate area.

The needy man can taste the fruit and doesn't mind the bit of mud now on it from the ground. Picking it up, he can't help but grow a smirk at his capture. Brushing the crisp little apple on the chest of his vest, he turns for the holy barrier and its safety. Lifting the food to his opening mouth, his eyes blink in awareness of more than apples as Eber stands in front of that barrier of safety.

Nearing one of the church's windows, Kasimir sees the figure blocking Biagio's return. A sick little smirk curls his lips.

Calmly, he stands watching Biagio unblinkingly. There is no motion or word between them. Biagio, while waiting for the General to make a move or threat, swallows what spit his dry throat can afford. "…Take a bite."

The man's eyes widen at the command. Does the Commander toy or mock him? Biagio has no clue Eber's intent by the words, the man's dead stare unrevealing of the thoughts behind it. Slowly, Biagio moves the apple to his mouth and bites. The juice sprays and feels like a waterfall plunging through his lips, down his throat. The taste filling his empty stomach much as the fiber itself. His dreamy eyes refocus on the nightmare of what is around him.

In a flash, he drops the apple and draws his daggers once more, lunging for the soldier. Not moving, Eber waits until the man is right in front of him, suddenly disappearing before the man, to reappear behind him. Grabbing onto his coat, Eber yanks his body and throws him across the street. Past Lorelei, Koza and his fellow soldier, Biagio crashes into the covered boardwalk of a business, slamming against the shop's wall.

"Ooo... that will not help the apple go down." Lorelei chuckles, her head bobbing as she stands in her own little twisted world, Koza casually glancing down to her, happy to see that world from the outside.

The sound of chaos summons undead. They rush for Biagio, his skin the shiny red apple, and his blood its juice down their throats. Shrieks and growls ring as the untoten crowd, pushing at each other to have the first bite. Snapping to his wits, Biagio slashes his blades, cutting ones that come close while they cut at each other in dominance over the prey. At once, the beings halt, their animal senses detecting a dominance that creates pause among them. No deep roar, no threatening growl, Eber's presence is menace as he climbs the steps to the porch of the building. The creatures part, letting him through to Biagio. Growing gumption, one of the alphas of the undead, jerks with a growl toward Eber. It is a motion returned by a cold manner and stare from the Commander on the creature, thereby forcing the thing to yield in its challenge to the other alpha.

Grunting, Biagio staggers to a stance, lurching his blades back to defence. Stabbing his own knives into Biagio's clothes, Eber grips his claws in the man's coat. He slams him against the wall of the building, smacking out a grunt of pain, the hit having more force behind it from something less than human. The solid wood breaking, Biagio's blades drop from his hands at the collision. With his senses shaking back into his head as Eber moves his grip to get a better hold of the other man, Biagio's hands land on the broken wall behind him, his palms being pierced by shards of wood.

The man's weight equates nothing to the Nachzherer, his life a toy, Eber heaves him from the deck out into the muddy street in the rain. Landing with an aching yell of pain, Biagio skids along in the mud until coming to a stop behind a mound of mud his body has built in front of him. Flopping his hands, he pulls them more under him, gritting his teeth.

Watching Eber step off the boardwalk into the rain, Koza and the soldiers stay silent and at a distance. Biagio has not been liked by any during this trip, but Eber's reasons for preying on him now are to do with Kasimir. If the Holy Man were to lose his only follower here, his only source of sustaining ego and superiority, then his conversion to Eber's side will be that much easier… and quicker. Where Koza observes with quiet disfavor for methods he knows Eber will never change, Lorelei smiles at the same sight, that of Biagio crawling through the mud as he's hunted by the General coming at his back. Not a smile, there is also no pity from Kasimir, staring out the window, watching his former devotee coming to the end of his life.

Hearing the sound of Eber's riding boots sinking in the muck with each step, Biagio knows he is now a reach away. As Eber begins that reach down to the man's back, Biagio rolls from his belly, stabbing the last sharp thing he has, one of the strips of wood from the broken building into Eber's chest like a stake. Jerking at the sudden attack, Koza's eyes widen and jaw drops while Ermanno and Thayer flinch at the same sight. Biagio's teeth grind and face scrunches as he pushes the piece of wood deep as his weakened strength can. In Eber's dark eyes are surprise and pain, but as the seconds pass, the only thing in them fades to a lifeless stare down on Biagio. Eber's small quiver of his lip over a fang stills as his face falls loose. Slowly, the Commander's body leans, finally dropping to the mud, the rain already washing at the puddle of blood forming under him.

"Merda," Ermanno utters almost half-mindedly, in shock.

"He killed the Commander! He did it!" Thayer yelps.

Hearing his men, Koza's thoughts start to come back from the fog, enough to realize the voice that has stayed silent. With a blink, he turns his focus down to Lorelei. Her pink lips parted and blue spheres widely staring, her brows curve. While the men wear surprise, Koza sees her wear... pain.

Starting to laugh, Biagio begins to climb to his feet over Eber. Swaying to a better stance, Biagio's chuckle stays strong. "...Lorelei?" Koza calls to her, his voice a haze at the edge of her mind as her body moves forward, coming down the steps of the building's footpath. Watching her step into the rain, Koza begins to feel strongly for her. What Eber and she truly were to each other was hard for him to understand, or any for that matter. She is a woman who loves herself, and he was a man who loved no one, yet between them, Koza saw something he knew existed despite their natures.

"...Eber?" her usual low voice of a woman sounds weaker in a tone almost that of a younger her.

Each small step she takes through the rain, the water falls over her, trickling down her hair, her clothes, her skin. The untoten look to her, the movement catching their attention, yet the scent of her human blood remains hidden under the wire vine. Biagio grins about his victory, towards Lorelei as she makes her way closer.

IIis chuckle quieting, Biagio's attention is pulled to Lorelei. Seeing her confused upset, he smiles. "You want to be stabbed in the heart next Gypsy?" Seeing the man mock her, Koza begins to draw his sword preparing to protect her.

Lorelei's eyes drift from the motionless Eber up to Biagio, her ears beginning to hear his threat, his snicker. She begins to see that egotistical smile of his. Lorelei's inhumanity slowly shows as a growl gradually rises. What drops Biagio's grin, is the fact that growl does not come from her lips, though they snarl the same, but the sounds of growls and deep throated rumbles are coming from around her body, spreading away from her. Steadily, Biagio watches as dark shadows grow from her, from the dark places around the street, the cracks and corners of buildings. Claws and fangs form in the shadows as they crawl across the puddles, growing in size as the drops of rain ripple their images. The shadow beasts snarl as they rise, some climbing in height around the untoten. The undead jerk and back from the shade creatures, instinct telling them this woman is a dominance all her own. Biagio starts to pant, his eyes widening as he begins to fear what he has summoned. "I am going to tear this village apart, and bury you under it." Lorelei's voice returns to its heavy depths as the shadows roar and extend their claws.

The soldiers gawk, awaiting the chaos to begin when their expressions of glee and fear abruptly shift back to the shock from before, as they see Eber come to stand behind Biagio. Seeing the Commander rise over the man's shoulder, Lorelei's fire to war douses instantly, her lips parting as she too simply stares in surprise. Dreading to learn what has changed the mood, Biagio slowly turns to see Eber before him. Eber's fangs bearing for a moment with his words. In the midst of the blink of his wide eyes, Biagio lets out a gurgle as Eber grips the man's throat. Choking, Biagio grabs at Eber's hand when the soldier aims the large piece of wood used to pierce his chest and stabs it deep into the side of his neck. The sounds of spurts mix with his gargles as blood spits out of the wound, Eber pushing the stake further in.

Letting go, Eber's wide hand flexes and claws come off Biagio, letting the man fall dead before him. Looking up from the body, the cold rain strings Eber's black hair along his face, his eyes darker than the sky above. He looks over the sight of undead, gathering to watch the conflict, looking to his men, Koza standing ready with the draw of his sword while Ermanno and Thayer stare behind him. Finally, his black eyes set on Lorelei and they start to change. The onyx color recedes from the whites of his eyes, returning his gaze to its usual amount of lifelessness.

Stepping over Biagio, he comes down the street, passing undead who watch him with no desire to interfere. Ermanno steps down to the muddy street, meeting Eber. With his eyes shifting from Biagio on ahead to the Commander, he pleads in a fashion taken over by inhumanity. He bares his wide fangs and twitches the bridge of his nose, the tension in his body easy to see in his posture. Being asked like an animal, Eber answers in kind, a low rumble coming from his throat as he nods to Biagio's body. With permission to eat another's kill, Ermanno rushes towards the dead man. Hurrying down the steps, Thayer passes Koza with a small glance of something akin to regret. His hunger building the same as Ermanno's has over the days, the smell of fresh blood spilling into the puddles below Biagio's body forces the young man into his own animal want.

Reaching the body with other untoten, Ermanno snaps a bite at the nearest one about to feed. Growling at those wanting to come closer. Careful of the second Lieutenant's hunger, Thayer makes his way submissively as Ermanno buries a bite into Biagio and eats. Koza forces a swallow, witness to others' hungers, always ripping away any appetite he may have.

Halting, Eber stands before Lorelei, his eyes lightly moving over her. Amid the rumbles of thunder above, the sounds of rain hitting buildings and puddles, the sounds of growls of undead around them, she drifts off into her own world of silent thought. Her lids calmly blink over the bright blue as she reaches a slim hand up to his chest. Moving her fingers, she brushes through fabric to see the wound of the stake that had been stabbed into his heart.

Her calm blinks bring her gaze back up to Eber, searching his face, his lips before connecting them to hers. Koza stands frozen by the past few minutes, now this. The Gypsy is not teasing, she is not at play in seduction or manipulation. Eber is a man of little reaction and his nature holds even being kissed by a beautiful woman. His normal coldness is present, until Lorelei's free hand raises, lightly gripping around the hilt of Romhild. Her fingers wrap the handle of the blade and steadily a change is seen in Eber. From tolerating her touch, he begins to welcome it, setting a hand to her lower back and pulling her more against him. Gradually, through the confusion of what he sees, Koza starts to hear what his disheveled mind likens to a sound of metal, something akin to a drawn out vibration in steel. It is the familiar sound he heard back in the woods when Eber threatened to drown the little girl. The same sound Koza noted when Lorelei touched that sword back then.

"Lorelei," Eber calls down to her quietly, his usual chilled manner much warmer. Brushing her mat of wet hair in her face against his cheek, she moves back, letting go of Romhild. At once, his eyes on her fade to their normal lifelessness again. "Inside, now." The usual coldness returns.

Keeping watch of the distracted untoten, Koza pushes his blade back into its sheath as Eber and Lorelei pass by him.

Following the Commander and the Woman back into the tavern Inn, Koza steps inside and shuts the door, latching it.

Unbuckling his sword belt, Eber hands the weapon over to Lorelei a stride behind him as he aims for the bar. Taking the blade, she finds a seat in one of the chairs, slanting the sword against her leg. There is a moment of relief in Eber's expression of pain from his injury, once the sword is in her hands.

The whole thing is striking Koza odd, seeing changes in Eber's demeanor, in his personality as the sword leaves his hands into hers. It is all confusing for the young captain. Nearing the Commander at the bar, Koza silently observes him for a time, seeing the wear on him from the pierce to his heart.

"Commander?"

"...Yes, Koza?"

"How did you get up?" The quietness from him spreads to Eber and Lorelei. "I know little about the creatures we are, but what I do know, is that a pierce of the heart kills the undead." He glances to Lorelei. "I do not understand." He returns to Eber. "Biagio stabbed your heart... Did he not?"

Seeing his befuddlement, Lorelei states her answer bluntly. "Perhaps it is not your place to understand, Koza." Her hand lifting to the hilt of the sword, her hold keeping it close to her.

Hearing the bland honesty, he also hears the slight gentleness she tried to convey, her favor for him showing in that small difference. Respectful of that favor, Koza nods. "I see."

"You have always been reliable, Koza." The Captain turns to Eber's plain statement. "You have come so far from that boy who needed me... I am proud of you."

Blinking, Koza begins to gawk, raising a worried hand up towards Eber's arm. "Commander, are you well?" Fear in his voice.

Almost a show of awareness in his strange nature in a breath out, Eber sets an arm on the brace of the bar. "Long ago, when I was a younger man, I faced a death I had no opportunity to return from as we all did in the mountains." Koza holds back the slightest word, knowing Eber has never been one to talk of tails. To hear anything about the man's past was more rare than a lunar eclipse. "Lorelei took measures to save me." Koza looks to the woman, once again, the long sound of a metal ping vibrating from under her soft grasp on the sword. "Biagio did not pierce my heart, because in my chest is not where my heart is."

At once, Koza's gawking stare blinks down to Lorelei in the chair, and the sword against her legs. "...Your heart is in the sword?"

"Bound to it." At that, the Captain is granted understanding for Eber's years of favor for that blade, his almost need for it to never leave him, its importance to him. "When it is in Lorelei's hands, under her touch, I can feel it once more as though it is returned to my chest."

Putting his own sense to the matter, Koza smiles warmly, looking between them. "Because you love her." He states.

"Because it was her magic that put it there."

"Oh." Koza's romantics dashed by Eber's more straightforward facts.

"...And because, I love her." Lorelei's eyes slowly lower from his, it is something she already knows, something Koza at first thinks she should be smiling to hear aloud, then realizes it is only these few times now in their lives she would hear it. Only these times when that sword is in her grasp, times when he is affected by its power that he remembers he once loved someone. It makes a sickly feeling between them all as Koza sees those thoughts in her usually bright blue eyes, lowering dimly to the blade she holds. In this pass of time, when his emotions cannot just be felt, but thought about, Eber's dark eyes show their own regrets, the freedom of pain, sadness, and affection something so strange to see gloss over them.

Feeling the weight of his own part in the story, all leaves Koza's face, but his seriousness. "I swear I will never tell a soul of this."

Those emotions drifting from Lorelei, Eber looks to Koza. "...I trust you." Knowing his words are more free while the sword sets in Lorelei's hands, Koza takes the remark to his own heart.

In the tavern, Koza sits quietly in a chair at a table while Ermanno paces, as every twitching muscle in his body screams for a violent activity in which to take part. Whilst Eber sits with eyes closed, resting in his seat or asleep. Lorelei wonders which it is as she leans over in front of his face, her long hair falling almost in his lap.

Coming to the table, Koza holds a steaming plate of food with towels wrapped around his hand in huge bundles. The image bringing a smirk to her pink lips, of him dressed like a military cook with the tavern's butcher's apron tied tightly around his narrow waist. He sets the plate down on the table, displaying it with his hands. "I hunted some more fish from the river nearby, Madam." He smiles at her. "This is your share, baked to flaky perfection as usual," he boasts.

Pleased, Lorelei picks up the fork and stabs for her first bite to cool off with a blow from her lips. "Someday, you will make some girl a wonderful wife, Koza." She slips the bite past her lips.

"Thank you." He nods, then hears what she said. "Wait-"

"Commander!" Thayer calls as he enters the tavern in slight haste. All turn to the young man, Eber opening his eyes to watch him come closer.

"Oh, he was awake after all." Lorelei chews behind a bent finger, looking on Eber.

"Kasimir wishes to discuss your terms, Sir."

KAPITEL XXVIII

Mjerovjec – Of Ukrainian origin. A person who when they were alive, blasphemed their church or had behaved as a monster, will become this sort of undead. Supposedly having a purple face, it was known to be awake from midnight until the third crow of a rooster in the morning. Having a fixation with poppy seeds, one could lure the beast back to its grave by placing food in a trail. One who turns from God to bargain with the Devil will be destined to become a Mjerovjec.

Outside the church, Kasimir passes the courtyard. Untoten gather, smelling the human blood and seeing it leave its sanctity. Turning on his heel, Kasimir moves to make another stride back and forth when the undead begin to part. Snarling, they bite at each other as they push each other to clear a path for Eber as he comes through them.

Kasimir halts, still close to the church doors as Eber stops at the gate to the church yard. "You wish to speak with me?" he asks, folding his arms over the twinge of pain still in his chest.

"Let me understand this correctly. You want my praise as the Head of the Church that you and your men are unlike these monsters?" He nods to the surrounding untoten, drooling at the smell of his blood. "You want me to commend you to Berin and the people of Loviturä? That you are no threat and instead are a source of protection?"

"Yes."

"And if I do not agree, you will leave me here to die?"

"Yes."

Kasimir weighs his options and thoughts over those options. "Get me the Hell out of here."

The carriage made its way to the familiar hills of the fortress city of Loviturä's borders. The horses pull through the dark of night by the portions of woods lit by Gypsy campfires. Kasimir watches Lorelei with a wary eye he has held open the entire trip home, whilst drowsily, Lorelei watches the sight of her people dancing and making lively with songs. Probably a new born baby, or marriage she thinks to herself, not having spent much time with them to know their lives. She is Romani by birth, true, but has never belonged among any people. Staring out the small window, Eber passes her view on Cerny and her attention shifts, trailing after him.

As King Berin readies himself for a plush night's rest in his chambers, a servant raps on the large gold encrusted door. "What is it?!" Berin barks, answering the door in his robe and nightgown with frilly sleeves that stuck out from the robe.

"The Head of the Church, Ambrozij Kasimir has returned. He wishes to speak with you."

Berin considers his level of fatigue and weighs it against Kasimir's level of power from the church and its devoted followers and decides, "Tell him I'm coming."

Kasimir sits patiently at the long table in the bleak and cold room used for political advisement. He sits staring at the stone acquired in Hieb as it rests on the table before him. He is a sullen quiet while Eber stands at the end of the table with folded arms, young Captain Koza at his side. Two servants push the two doors open and Berin enters with arms out in a more lavish robe, one meant better for receiving guests. "Kasimir! How good to see you my friend," his voice booms in its usual low pitch and thick Bohemian accent as nearly all of his soldiers have.

Kasimir raises his hand to the man and stays in his seat. "Please, I desire no gripping embraces." Berin has an inner thought of anger that Kasimir has enough wealth and manipulation of his own subjects that he can demand the King's silence and get it. "My body has been through enough punishment."

Dismissing the hate, Berin sits with false concern. "What has happened?!"

"The village of Hieb is decimated."

"No!"

"An army of undead swept through it like an unforgiving flood."

"What happened when you arrived?"

"The creatures attacked us. General Soldat and his men were killed."

Berin sits back in his seat, "but he stands here!"

Kasimir precedes in comfort with his deception, "he and his men returned from the dead."

Berin slaps his wide hand down on the table. "I always thought of you as a sturdy bastard Eber, but this amazes even me!" Eber's expression is unchanging as he stares down at Berin, Koza glancing to the Commander with nearly a roll of his eyes. "And what should be done now about Eber and his men?" he asks Kasimir.

After a considering pause at what is about to come out of his mouth, Kasimir continues, "They should be accepted as assets to your empire."

"Truly? You, his Holy Highness accept what Eber and his men are?"

"If it had not been for the Commander and his men, I would not have lived to return to Loviturä," he states as if each word hurts.

The happy filled joy it would have brought Berin to hear of Kasimir's demise is reflected in his crooked glance up at Eber. "Well, thank God," he lowers his gaze to the table.

"Now, if you will excuse me," Kasimir rises from his seat. "I have had a very long trip and wish it to end." He passes a satisfied glance to Eber as he turns to leave. "Goodnight." Berin and the General watch Kasimir walk, tucking his precious stone in his arms as he calls to the servants outside to open the large doors.

"Your Holiness?" Koza stops Kasimir at the door.

"What?" He turns.

"What is that stone you brought from Hieb anyway?"

After a pause, he answers the young man. "It is a Sledovik." And with that, he turns and leaves the room.

KAPITEL XXIX

Coming down the grand staircase of the castle into the courtyard, Koza notes Thayer and Ermanno returning the coach and horses to the stables far off.

Halting with a bounce on the last step, he looks from the men, to Lorelei as she awaits with Cerny, nuzzling the stallion's velvet nose, the horse adoring it. Eber passes her, casually taking the reins from her.

"Madam Zima?" Koza calls.

"Yes, Koza?"

"You have given us so many answers through all this. May I ask one more question?"

Eber mounts the horse, Cerny taking a step or two in place. "Of course." She smiles.

"What is a Sledovik?"

Seeing the young Captain has finally come to learn more about what Kasimir traveled for, she smirks. "It is a holy stone some say has been marked by Jesus Christ."

Eber turns up from her to Koza, having listened to the answer he figured she would undoubtedly have. Koza gawks at the Commander. "That is what we went through all of this for? What he found worth risking his life for?"

"I would not be surprised if you see him using that stone as he has used many things to re-instill his holy reign here… Who would doubt a man of God with so many things of God's?" In her tease, Koza hears perhaps an experience of the past, one Eber perhaps shares the memory of as he looks from the Captain down to Lorelei, holding out his hand. Accepting it, she welcomes her place behind him as Eber lifts her onto Cerny. "Goodnight, Koza." She smiles playfully. "This has been fun."

"Watch Ermanno and Thayer while they put away the horses." Eber turns Cerny for the gates. "I do not need them eating a stable boy." Koza's eyes widen with the thoughts he had not considered. "I can do without the disrepute." Leaving the yard, Cerny makes his way as Koza scrambles a little to get to the stables in a hurry.

In the hills by the outer walls of Lovblturä, Eber guides Cerny through familiar trees at the outskirts of the gypsy camp. Their vardos and tents still alive and lit by fires and lamps, burning in windows and pits. People sitting and talking, roasting food over the fires while men and women dance in celebration of their localized party.

The rock of Cerny's steps, his smooth pace helping remind Lorelei of her tiredness, she sways with his motion, gradually laying her head to Eber's back. Slowly, what little awareness her sleepy body has, makes her conscious of how soft the soldier's coat is against her face as she nestles against his back, how loose her grip is getting around his waist. Lifting up, her eyes catch Eber's as he checks on her behind him. She shakes her head lightly and straightens, a show that she is now awake and his shoulder blade is not needed.

Her gaze casting out into the night of dancing gypsies, she smirks. "Azzo's wife must have had another son."

Cerny arrives at Lorelei's little part of the camp far into the woods away from all else. Dismounting, she makes her way into the bender tent.

Trailing behind her, Eber sets the bag she had brought on the journey to one of the small tables. She lowers to her knees by the fire pit, lighting flames to the dead wood. The light and warmth already spreading through the fabric walls of the tent, she moves to the couple ropes by a post, opening the vent for the smoke to climb up and out.

Watching her actions, Eber simply observes her. "Home at last," she breathes, dropping her hands to her hips.

"Thank you." She turns up to him by the table. "Your assistance was useful."

She grows a smirk. "Yes, well." She sways, her hands staying to her hips as she twists them. "We have not decided your payment for my assistance yet." She stops before him, leaning towards him as he still simply stares.

"What do you want from me?"

"Hmm? What do I want?" She sets a finger to her lip. "You tell me, Commander. What would a grown woman want with a handsome man who owes her and is only a couple," she pauses, glancing back to her bed nearby. "A few steps away from her bed?" Her smirk holds on his dead eyes.

"I would have expected something more, costly." He answers in a bland humor.

Her smirk becoming something more sincere she then tries to hide with a twist of her body, she says, "on second thought, consider my help just that, help." She ventures closer back to the fire and in her tone he can hear a slow shift as she stares into the flames. "You owe me nothing, Soldier."

A silence grows and gradually, Eber turns from the sight of her. Aimed for the entrance of the tent, he has a moment of thought and halts. Unmoving, he stares at the entrance, then turns back towards her. Capturing the corner of her eye, she blinks to him as he comes to her side. His lifeless eyes hold on her. Lifting a hand, he holds it out for hers. She cautiously sets one in his and he brings it to Romhild's hilt. Watching him gently curl her fingers under his around the sword's handle, her eyes rise to his as they begin to grow that lost life from so long ago. The hum of metal beginning to sound in a soft pitch from the blade.

"...I am sorry." Her brows curve, her lips parting. "Sorry for what was taken from us."

A breath jerking in her throat, she answers, "I am the one who took it."

"To save me," he says with forgiveness and warmth. "I will always love you, but I will not always be able to feel I do." His grip over her hand on Romhild tightens. "For that, I want to say I am sorry." She stands wanting to say much, but listens instead. "That is what I owe you, Lorelei." There is a pain in her eyes, one he knows he causes. He lifts his hand from hers on the sword, letting her draw her hand back to her, the emotionless expression returning to his dark eyes as she does. She gathers herself, putting her hands together at her waist. "Goodnight, Lorelei." He bends a soft kiss to her cheek.

It is something without love, or intention than just that, a kiss to her skin, but in that strangeness, it means oddly much to her, that he does it when his heart is not connected. Perhaps a sign of the chance to see more of who he used to be in who he is. Something for her to reflect on, watching him leave.

The End

Thank you for reading.
I hope you enjoyed this piece of fiction. Now that you've finished the journey,
please consider leaving an honest review of the work.
Feedback helps me grow as a writer and it helps others find this story.

Author Info

@SaydaHope - Twitter

@SaydaHope - Instagram

SaydaHope - YouTube